Luke shoved Laura down behind the car, his hand covering her head. "Friends of yours?"

"I don't know," she said on a gasp of air, the shock of her words telling him she was being honest. "What's going on?"

"You tell me." He lifted his head an inch. And was rewarded with another round of rifle fire. "Somebody doesn't like you being here, sweetheart."

She tried to peek around the car's bumper, but he held her down. Glaring up at him, she whispered, "I don't know what you're talking about. Are you sure they aren't shooting at you?"

"That is a possibility," he said on a growl. "I've made a lot of enemies lately."

"Anybody in particular?"

Luke thought about the laundry list of sins he'd committed in the name of grief. "We don't have that long. I have to get you out of here."

She seemed to like that idea. "So...how do you plan to do that?"

Books by Lenora Worth

Love Inspired Suspense

Deadly Texas Rose
A Face in the Shadows
Heart of the Night
Code of Honor
Risky Reunion
Assignment: Bodyguard
The Soldier's Mission

Steeple Hill

After the Storm
Echoes of Danger
Once Upon a Christmas
  "'Twas the Week
    Before Christmas"

Love Inspired

***When Love Came to Town*
***Something Beautiful*
***Lacey's Retreat*
Easter Blessings
  "The Lily Field"
†*The Carpenter's Wife*
†*Heart of Stone*
†*A Tender Touch*
Blessed Bouquets
  "The Dream Man"
*A Certain Hope
*A Perfect Love
*A Leap of Faith

Christmas Homecoming
Mountain Sanctuary
Lone Star Secret
Gift of Wonder
The Perfect Gift
Hometown Princess

**In the Garden
†Sunset Island
*Texas Hearts

LENORA WORTH

has written more than forty books, most of those for Steeple Hill. She has freelanced for a local magazine, where she wrote monthly opinion columns, feature articles and social commentaries. She also wrote for the local paper for five years. Married to her high school sweetheart for thirty-five years, Lenora lives in Louisiana and has two grown children and a cat. She loves to read, take long walks, sit in her garden and go shoe shopping.

THE
SOLDIER'S
MISSION

LENORA WORTH

Steeple
Hill®

Published by Steeple Hill Books™

STEEPLE HILL BOOKS

Steeple Hill®

Recycling programs for this product may not exist in your area.

ISBN-13: 978-0-373-44421-2

THE SOLDIER'S MISSION

Copyright © 2010 by Lenora H. Nazworth

www.SteepleHill.com

Printed in U.S.A.

"But by sorrow of the heart the spirit is broken."
—*Proverbs* 15:13

To my son Kaleb—a true heart hunter.

ONE

He'd had the dream again.

The stifling desert air burned hot, dirty and dry. The acrid smell of charred metal and scorched wires mixed with the metallic, sickly sweet smell of blood all around him. The sound of rapid-fire machine guns mingled with the screams of pain as, one by one, the men in his unit fell. He saw the horror of a landmine exploding against the jagged rocks of the craggy mountainside where they'd been penned down for forty-eight hours. One misstep and three of his men gone in a flash of searing fire and ear-shattering explosions. The others were taken out as the insurgents fought to the finish.

Then, the eerie sound of a deathly silence as the shooting stopped…and even after all of Luke's efforts to save his wounded men, the moans and cries for help eased away…until there was nothing left but scorched dust lifting out over the rocks.

He was the only man left standing. But he wasn't alone on that mountain. And he knew he'd be dead before dusk.

He'd jolted awake, gasping for air, a cold sweat covering his body, his hands shaking, grasping for his machine gun.

Luke "Paco" Martinez sat up and pushed at his damp hair then searched for the glowing green of the digital clock. 6:00 a.m. Old habits died hard. And a good night's sleep was always just beyond his reach.

Barefoot, his cotton pajama bottoms dragging on the cool linoleum of the tiny trailer's floor, Luke went straight to the coffeepot and hit the brew button. And while he waited for the coffee, he stared at the lone bottle of tequila sitting on the window seal.

Stared and remembered the dream, the nightmare, that wouldn't let him find any rest.

Looking away from the tempting bottle of amber liquid, he instead focused on the distant mountains. The desert and mountains here in Arizona were a contrast against the rocky, unforgiving mountains of Afghanistan. Even though this high desert country was harsh and brutal at times, he could find comfort in the tall prickly saguaros and occasional thickets of Joshua trees and pinon pines growing all around his home. Here, he could run toward the mesas and the mountains and find solace, his questioning prayers echoing inside his head while his feet pounded on the dirt, his mind going numb with each step, each beat of his racing heart. *Why was I spared, Lord?*

In the dream, Luke screamed his own rage as he moved headlong into the fray, his M4 carbine popping what seemed like a never-ending round on the insurgents hidden in the hills.

In the dream, he always woke up before they killed him.

And because he did wake up and because he was alive to relive that horrible day over and over, he stared at the liquor bottle while he drank his coffee and told himself he could get through this.

Focus on the mountains, Paco.

That's what his grandfather had told him the day he'd come here to wrestle his soul back from the brink. Focus on the mountains.

He was better now, six months after coming home to Arizona. He was getting better each and every day, in spite of the nightmares. He'd even gone on a few short-term missions for CHAIM, the secret organization he'd been a member of since before he'd joined the army.

He was better now. No more drunken binges, no more fights in restaurants and bars. Not as much pain. The army might not believe that, but his fellow CHAIM agents did, thankfully.

He'd be okay, Luke told himself. He just needed a little more time. And a lot more prayers.

So he drained his coffee and put on his running clothes and headed out into the early morning chill of the ever-changing desert, away from the little trailer that was his home now, away from the nightmares and the memories.

And away from that tempting bottle of golden relief.

She couldn't get his voice out of her head.

Laura Walton thought about the man she'd come to the desert to find. The man everyone was worried about. The man who, a few weeks ago, had called the CHAIM hotline in the middle of the night.

"My father died in Vietnam," the grainy, low voice said over the phone line. "My brother was wounded in Desert Storm. He's in a wheelchair now. And I just got back from Afghanistan. Lost my whole unit. Lost everyone. I think I need to talk to somebody."

Laura had been on call that night, volunteering to man the hotline that CHAIM held open for all of its operatives, the world over.

But only one call had come to the Phoenix hotline on that still fall night. One call from a man who was suffering a tremendous amount of survivor's guilt.

Laura understood this kind of guilt. She didn't have survivor's guilt, but her own guilt ate away at her just the same. She'd lost a patient recently. A young patient who'd taken his own life. She'd failed the teenager.

She didn't want to fail Luke Martinez.

The soldier's tormented words, spoken with such raw pain, had stayed with her long after the man had hung up.

Which he did, immediately after confessing that he needed to talk.

It hadn't been easy convincing her CHAIM supervisors in Phoenix to let her go through case files and match the man to the words, then come to this remote spot near the Grand Canyon to find Luke "Paco" Martinez. Nor had it been easy taking time away from the clinic where she worked as a counselor to Christians suffering all sorts of crises.

But this crisis trumped all the rest. This man needed help. Her help. And somehow, in her guilt-laden mind, Laura had decided this was a sign from God to redeem her. She had to find this man. So she'd traced his cell number to this area.

So here she sat in a dump of a roadside café called The Last Stop, hoping she'd find the illusive Paco Martinez, also known as "The Warrior". Fitting name, Laura thought now as she dared to take another sip of the too-dark, too-strong coffee the stoic old man at the counter had poured for her. While she relied on the tip she'd received about Luke coming here every morning for breakfast, Laura went back over his file.

The army neither confirmed nor denied it, but Luke Martinez was reported to be some sort of Special Forces soldier—a shadow warrior—as they were often called. And while the elite Delta Force didn't put a lot of emphasis on rank, preferring to use code names or nicknames instead of stating rank, from what she could glean Martinez was a hero who'd been the lone survivor of a highly secretive mission to rescue two American soldiers trapped behind enemy lines in Afghanistan.

Everything about the mission had gone bad. Luke's team of men had been dropped by helicopter onto the mountain with orders to find the two soldiers and bring them home. After taking one outpost and locating the two badly beaten soldiers, Luke's team had made it back to the pickup spot to wait on a helicopter out. But the enemy had advanced behind them and taken out all of Luke's men, including the two his team has rescued. Things got fuzzy after that, but according to the rumors swirling around, The Warrior had managed not only to escape the men who tried to take him hostage, but he'd killed all of them in the process. And he refused to leave that mountain until the rescue team had recovered all of his men.

Except the one who'd seen all of them die. Luke Martinez had survived and for that, he was suffering mightily.

So he'd come home an unknown hero—that was the code of Special Forces—but Martinez didn't want to be a hero, didn't care that most would never know what he'd tried to do on that mountaintop. He was still in pain, still reeling from losing his team members. Deep inside, he was having a crisis. Post-traumatic stress over losing his men and for what he considered his failure—not bringing the stranded soldiers back safely.

That had caused a bout of serious drinking and many hours spent in jail cells and later with stress counselors and army specialists.

As well as CHAIM counselors such as Laura. His CHAIM team had stood by Luke, with one stipulation. He had to go to their remote retreat center in Ireland— Whelan Castle—for some serious debriefing and counseling sessions. And hopefully, to find some peace.

Luke had agreed. And he'd improved after his three months in Ireland. Then he'd come home to Arizona to rest. But he'd been called out on a mission in Texas to help Shane Warwick, known as The Knight, guard and protect prominent Texas socialite Katherine Atkins.

According to the official report, Luke had done a good job backing up Warwick and they'd brought down not only the woman who was trying to kill Katherine, but a ruthless oil-smuggling cartel to boot.

But this late night phone call had come *after* Luke had returned from Texas.

Which brought Laura back to the here-and-now. And this stand-on-its-own-legs coffee.

Laura motioned to the old man behind the counter, finding the courage to ask him the one question she'd come here to ask. "Excuse me, sir, do you know a man named Luke Martinez?"

The old man with the silver-black braid going down his back didn't respond to her question. Instead he just stared at her with such opaque eyes, Laura felt as if the man could see into her very soul.

"Sir?"

Finally the man shuffled up to the counter, his tanned, aged skin reminding Laura of one of the craggy mountain faces beyond the desert. He wore a white cotton button-down shirt that hung like a tunic on his body, giving him the look of someone on their way to a fiesta.

Before she could ask the question again, he leaned forward, his frown as stand-up as the coffee. "Would you like some pie with that coffee?"

Surprised, Laura shook her head. "Ah, no thanks. I had a granola bar in the car. About the man I'm looking for—"

"Can't help you there," the old man replied, turning before Laura could finish the sentence.

But the old man didn't need to help her. The rickety screen door flapped open and she felt the hair on the back of her neck rising, felt his eyes on her even before she looked into the aged mirror running along the back wall and saw his reflection there. Completely paralyzed with confusion and doubt, she lowered her gaze then heard that distinctive voice without turning to face him.

"I'll take some pie, Grandfather." He advanced toward Laura. "And while you're getting my pie, I'll ask this pretty lady why she's trying so hard to find me."

Luke stood perfectly still, his senses on edge while he analyzed the woman sitting at the counter. Her brown hair fell around her face and shoulders in soft waves. She wore a sensible beige lightweight sweater, a faded pair of jeans and hiking boots. Interesting. He could smell her perfume, a mixture of sweet flowers and vanilla. Nice.

Then she turned to face him and Luke's gaze caught hers, the deep blue of her eyes reminding him of a mountain sky just before dusk. The look in those eyes amused him even while it destroyed him. She was afraid of him. And she probably had good reason.

"Mr. Martinez?"

Her voice was soft but firm. She quickly recovered from her first glimpse, Luke noted. She got points for that, at least. Most people just ran the other way when he scowled at them.

"Paco," he replied. "That's what everyone around here calls me."

She reached out a dainty hand, her nails clean and painted with a clear sparkle of polish, her fingers devoid of rings. "I'm Laura Walton."

Luke took her hand for a second then let it go, her perfume warming his fingers. "Okay. You already know me and now I know your name. Why are you here?"

She leaned in then glanced around the nearly empty diner. "I'm... from CHAIM."

He liked the way she pronounced it—"Chi-Im", with the *CH* sounding more like a *K* using the Hebrew enunciation. He did not like that she was here.

Luke pushed a hand through his hair and sat down beside her, the weight of his body causing the old spinning stool to squeak and groan. "Coffee, Grandfather, please. And two pieces of buttermilk pie."

"I don't want pie."

Luke didn't argue with her. "Make that one piece and two forks, Grandfather." He waited for his pretending-not-to-be-interested grandfather to bring the requested food. Then he shoved one fork at her and took his own to attack the creamy yellow-crusted pie. "Eat."

She looked down at the plate then picked up the fork. "I don't eat sweets."

"Try it."

Luke took his time eating his own side of the pie. Then he sipped the dark brew, his gaze hitting at hers in the old, pot-marked mirror running behind the cluttered counter. "Now, why are you here?"

She chewed a nibble of pie then swallowed, her eyes opening big while she slanted a gaze toward him. "One of your friends was concerned."

"I don't have a lot of friends."

"The Knight," she said on a low whisper.

"Just saw him a few weeks ago."

"I know. He wanted to make sure you were okay."

Luke knew she wasn't telling him the whole story. He'd talked to Shane Warwick two days ago. The man was crazy in love and making big plans for his upcoming Texas spring wedding. Shane was going to repeat the vows he'd spoken in England—to the same woman he'd married in England. He'd called Luke to invite him to the wedding but Shane had asked Luke how he was doing. Polite conversation or pointed inquiry?

"Who are you?" he asked, this time all the smile gone out of the question. "And don't lie to me, lady."

Laura swallowed down more coffee, hoping it would give her more courage. "I told you, I'm from CHAIM."

"Who really sent you?"

Laura couldn't hide the truth. "I...I came on my own. I mean, I got clearance to come but I asked to come and see you."

His smile was so quick and full of stealth, she almost missed it. But if he ever did really smile, Laura believed it would do her in for good. The man was an interesting paradox of good-looking coupled with dangerous and scary. His dark hair, longer than army regulations allowed since he was usually undercover, sliced in damp inky lines across his scarred face and around his muscled neck. His eyes were onyx, dark and rich and unreadable. His skin was as aged and marked as tanned leather. It rippled over hard muscle and solid strength each time he moved. He wore a black T-shirt and soft-washed jeans over battered boots. And he smelled fresh and clean, as if he'd just stepped out of a secret waterfall somewhere.

His gaze cut from her to the mirror, watching, always watching the door of the diner.

"Why did you feel you had to come and see me?"

Laura prided herself on being honest. So with a swallow and a prayer, she said, "Because you called me—on the CHAIM hotline—late one night. You said you needed someone to talk to. So I'm here."

Luke lowered his head, the shame of that phone call announcing how weak he'd felt that night. He'd had the dream again, maybe because he had just returned from Texas and more death and dishonesty. Maybe because he would always have the dream and he'd always feel weak and guilty and filled with such a self-loathing that it took his breath away and made him want to drink that whole bottle of tequila sitting on the windowsill.

"I shouldn't have called," he said, the words hurting and tight against his throat muscles. "You didn't have to come here, Ms. Walton. I'm fine now."

She went from being intimidated to being professional with the blink of her long lashes. "You didn't sound fine that night. I called Shane Warwick and he arranged permission for me to come and see you. I live in Phoenix."

Luke whirled on the stool, his face inches from hers. "Then go back to Phoenix and leave me alone."

"But...you...shouldn't be alone. I'm a counselor. You can trust me and you can talk to me about anything. Even if you've slipped up and had a drink—"

"Leave. Now," Luke said, grabbing her by the arm.

"But—"

"I haven't had a drink in four months and I don't need you here. All I need right now is to be left alone."

He saw the concern in her eyes, saw the hesitation in her movements. She wasn't going to leave without a fight.

Luke glanced toward his grandfather. The old man's face was set in stone, as always. But Luke could see the hope shining in the seventy-nine-year-old's black eyes.

He didn't want to disappoint his grandfather, but Luke didn't want this woman hovering over him, trying to get inside his head, either.

"I'll take you back to your car," he said, guiding her with a push toward the door.

Laura Walton shot a look at him over her shoulder. "I have to make sure you're ready to come back to CHAIM full-time now that you're back from the Middle East and out of the army."

"I'm ready," Luke said on a strained breath. Why had he dialed that number that night? Now he had trouble here in the form of a dark-haired female. A pretty, sweet-smelling woman with big blue eyes and an academic, analyzing mind. The worst kind.

"Could we have a talk?" she asked, digging her heels in with dainty force.

"We just had a talk and now we're done."

He had her out the door, the warmth of the morning sun searing them to the dirt-dry parking lot. "Where's your car?"

"Over there." She pointed to a small red economy car. "It's a rental. My car is in the shop."

Luke tugged her forward until they were beside the car. "Then you can be on your way back to the rental counter. Have a nice trip back to Phoenix."

She turned to stare up at him, her eyes so imploring and so blue, he had to blink.

And during that blink, a bullet ricocheted off the windshield of her car, shattering glass all around them in a spray of glittering white-hot slivers.

TWO

Paco shoved Laura down behind the car, his hand covering her head. "Friends of yours?"

"I don't know," she said on a gasp of air, the shock of her words telling him she was being honest. "What's going on?"

"You tell me." He lifted his head an inch. And was rewarded with another round of rifle fire. "Somebody doesn't like you being here, sweetheart."

She tried to peek around the car's bumper, but he held her down. Glaring up at him, she whispered, "I don't know what you're talking about. Are you sure they aren't shooting at you?"

"That is a possibility," he said on a growl. "I've made a lot of enemies lately."

"Anybody in particular?"

Paco thought about the laundry list of sins he'd committed in the name of grief. "We don't have that long. I have to get you out of here."

She seemed to like that idea. "So how do you plan to do that?"

"Good question." Paco pulled his sunglasses out of his T-shirt pocket and shoved them on then slowly lifted so he could scan the surrounding desert and mountains.

"If it's a sniper, we're stuck here. If we move, they could take us out in a split second. But if they're just using a twelve-gauge or some other sort of rifle, we might have a chance at making a run for the café."

"My windshield is shattered," she said, her tone sensible. "That means they could do the same to us if we move."

"True. But a moving target is a lot harder to pinpoint than a parked car."

"Maybe they weren't aiming at us."

Paco glanced around the empty parking lot. "We're the only customers right now."

"Your grandfather?"

"Doesn't have an enemy anywhere in the world." Paco held her there, the scent of her perfume merging with the scent of dirt and grim and car fumes. "And if I know my grandfather, he's standing at the door of the café with his Remington." He rolled over to pick up a rock. Then with a quick lift of his arm, he threw it toward the small porch of the rickety restaurant.

His grandfather opened the dark screen door then shouted. "One shooter, Paco. Coming from the west. Want me to cover you?"

Paco took his grandfather's age and agility into consideration. "Only if you don't expose yourself."

"I won't."

"Are you sure he can handle this?" Laura asked, her words breathy and low.

"Oh, yeah." Paco grabbed her, lifting her to face him. "Now listen to me. We're going to make a run for the porch. Grandfather will cover us. You'll hear gunshots but just keep running."

Fright collided with sensibility in her eyes. "What if I get shot?"

"I won't let that happen."

"But you can't protect me and yourself, too."

"Yes, I can," Paco said, images from his time in special ops swirling in slow motion in his head. "I can. But you have to stay to my left and you have to run as fast as you can."

"Okay. I ran track in college."

"Good. That's good. I need you to stay low and sprint toward that door on the count of three."

She did as he said, crouching to a start. Paco counted and prayed. "One, two, three."

And then they took off together while his grandfather stepped out onto the porch and shot a fast round toward the flash in the foothills about a hundred yards away. Paco put himself between her and the shooter and felt the swish of bullets all around his body. Then he pushed her onto the porch and into the door, holding it open for his grandfather to step back inside.

The old man quickly shut the door then turned to stare at Paco and Laura, his rifle held up by his side. "Would either of you care to explain this?"

Laura's gaze moved from the old man to Paco. "I don't know who's out there. As far as I know, no one wants *me* dead." Watching Paco, she could believe the man might have a few enemies—probably several heartbroken women among them. "What about you?" she asked, wondering what was going on inside his head.

His grandfather chuckled at that. "Only about half the population of Arizona, for starters."

"Thanks." Paco replied with a twisted grin. "Grandfather, I forgot my manners, what with being shot at and all. This is Laura Walton. She thinks I need her help."

"Do you?" the old man asked, putting his gun down to reach out a gnarled hand to Laura. "Nice to meet you. Sorry you almost got shot. I'm Wíago—Walter Rainwater."

"Nice to meet you, too," Laura said, her breath settling down to only a semi-rapid intake. The weirdness of the situation wasn't lost on her but she was too timid to shout out her true feelings. Turning back to Paco, she asked, "What do we do now?"

Paco didn't answer. Instead, he went through a door toward the back of the café then returned with a mean-looking rifle. "*You* wait here with Grandfather."

Walter put the Closed sign on the door. "It was a slow morning anyway."

"It's always a slow morning around here," Paco quipped. "Even when we aren't being shot at."

Laura twisted her fingers in Paco's sleeve. "What are you doing?"

"I'm going out there to track that shooter."

"But he might kill you."

"Always a chance, but don't worry about me too much. I think I can handle this."

Laura didn't know why it seemed so important to keep him safe. Maybe because she hadn't had a chance to get inside his head and help him over his grief. Or maybe because while he frightened her, he also intrigued her and she'd like to explore that scenario.

Shocked at her wayward thoughts, she chalked it up to being nearly killed and said, "Well, be careful. I have to give a full report on you."

"I'm used to having full reports done on me," he

replied, his dark eyes burning with a death wish kind of disregard. "If I bite the bullet, you can just tell the powers that be that I died fighting."

Laura ventured a glance at his grandfather and saw the worry in the old man's eyes. That same concern strengthened her spine and gave her the courage to reason with him. "But we don't know who you're fighting this time."

"I've never known who I've been fighting." Paco graced her with a long, hard stare before he pivoted and headed toward the back of the building. "Stay put and lock both doors. Don't come out until you hear me calling."

Paco crept through the flat desert, willing himself to blend in with the countryside. The black shirt wasn't very good camouflage but it would have to do. If he could make it around the back way and surprise the gunman, he'd have a chance of figuring out who was out there and why.

So he did a slow belly-crawl through the shrubs and thickets, careful to watch for snakes and scorpions. Stopping to catch his breath underneath a fan palm, he held still and did a scan of the spot where his grandfather had indicated the shooter might be hiding. A cluster of prickly pear cacti stood spreading about four feet high and wide alongside a cropping of Joshua trees centered on the rise of the foothills leading toward a small mesa. But Paco didn't see anything or anyone moving out there.

Thinking maybe the culprit was hiding much in the same way as he, Paco slid another couple of feet, careful to be as silent as possible. The sun had moved up in the sky and even though it was November, the desert's temperature had moved right along with it. Sweat beaded on his forehead and poured down his face. His shirt was now damp and dusty. He could taste the sand, feel it in his eyes. For a minute, he was back on that mountainside, waiting, just waiting for the enemy to make a move.

But fifteen minutes later, Paco hadn't seen any signs of human life in this desolate desert. So he threw a clump of rocks toward the thicket and waited for a hail of bullets to hit him.

Nothing.

Grunting, Paco lifted to a crouch, his gun aimed at the Joshua trees a few feet ahead. He was a trained sniper so he didn't think the other guy would stand a chance. But then, he'd been wrong before.

Laura hated the silence of this place.

Walter Rainwater didn't talk. Not at all. If she asked a question, he'd answer "Yes", "No" or "We'll wait for Paco."

She was tired of waiting for Paco. So she got up to look out the window for the hundredth time. "He should have been back by now."

A hand on her arm caused her to spin around. Tugging Laura toward a booth, Paco said, "We need to talk."

Surprised and wondering more than a little bit how he'd snuck up on her, she pulled a notebook from the shoulder bag she'd managed to hang on to in all the chaos. Maybe the episode outside had triggered something in Paco.

But she was wrong. "Put that away," he said, pushing

at the notebook. "We're not talking about me. I need to ask *you* a few questions. We have to figure out who's trying to kill you."

Laura took in his dirty shirt and the sweat beads on his skin. "Did you find someone?"

He shook his head, took the water his grandfather sat on the table. "No. Whoever was there is gone now. I found shell casings and tracks, footprints out toward the highway." Then he handed her a dirty business card. "I did find this."

Laura looked down at the piece of paper then gulped air. "That's one of my cards."

His smirk held a hint of accusation. "Yeah, saw your name right there on it. But nothing after that. I guess once we managed to get inside here, they left. But I don't think they dropped this card by accident. They wanted you to know they were here."

"But why?"

Instead of answering, he drank the water down, giving Laura plenty of time to take in his slinky, spiky bangs and slanted unreadable eyes while she wondered about why the shooter had left *her* business card.

He put the glass down and met her gaze head-on. "I think you know why. Ready to tell me the truth?"

"Me?" Shocked, Laura drew back, her head hitting the vinyl of the booth. "I told you as far as I know, no one's after me."

Paco leaned across the table, his expression as black as his eyes. "Yes, ma'am, someone is after you. Another inch and your rental car's windshield would still be intact. But you'd probably be dead." He sat back, his big hands centered against the aged oak of the table. "Now, think real hard and tell me if you've had any hard-case patients lately."

"None, other than you," she replied, the triumph she should have felt disappearing at the ferocious glare in his eyes.

"Look, lady, I didn't ask you to come here. And up until about an hour ago, no one cared about me or what I'm doing. This place is about as remote as you can get. So I figure someone tailed you here and waited for the right opportunity to shoot at you. And that means you've probably got an unstable client out there with an ax to grind. So quit insulting me and think real hard about some of the people you've counseled lately." He leaned over the table again, his tone soft and daring. "Besides me."

Laura stared across at him, wondering how he could stay so calm when they were sitting here with a possible sniper still on the loose. "I don't have a clue—"

"Think about it," he said in that deep, low voice that sent ripples of awareness down her spine. "How many people have you talked to in say, the last three or four months?"

"Too many to tell," she retorted. "I'd have to have access to my files."

"You mean by computer?"

"Yes." She tapped her big purse. "I didn't bring my laptop with me. Besides, I can't download every case history I have on file."

Paco pulled a slick phone out of his pocket. "What if I get us some help?"

"But no one has access to my patient files. That's confidential."

"I know someone who can break into those files."

She shook her head. "I can't allow that. My clients trust me."

"That won't matter if you're dead."

The man certainly cut right to the chase.

"Who are you going to call?"

"Kissie Pierre. You've probably heard of her. She keeps computer records on all the CHAIM agents and she keeps files on anyone who has any dealings with those agents. And that includes counselors."

"The Woman at the Well. But she can't help us with this type of thing."

"If you give her some names, she'll be able to crack your files and compare notes."

"Confidentially?"

"Yes, completely confidential, I promise."

"Legal?"

"As legal as we can make it. This is an emergency. But if you think you can remember without us going to that extreme then talk to me."

Laura preferred that method to hacking into private files. "Let me make a list of names. Maybe that will bring back some memories."

"Good." Paco grabbed her notebook. "Got a pen?"

She found a pen in her purse then handed it over to him. Walter passed by with phantom quietness, his rifle held at his chest. "Nobody coming to call. I think we're in the clear."

Paco looked at the door. "Keep an eye out, Grandfather. They might try to sneak up on us again."

Walter nodded, his solid presence a comfort to Laura.

Paco and his grandfather were close. She could tell by the respect Paco offered the old man and by the way they teased each other, both serious and stoic but with a trace of mirth in their eyes.

"Are you thinking?" Paco asked, his gaze cutting to the windows and the door. "We don't have much time. They might decide to come back for another visit. And bring friends along."

Laura sank back, terrified of that prospect. "I'm a pastoral counselor. I mostly deal with church members with marriage problems, those who've lost a loved one, or teenagers who are going through angst. Things like that. And CHAIM agents and workers, of course."

"Of course. Anyone who stands out in your mind?"

She put her head down, bringing her right arm up to settle on the table, then leaned her chin against her fist, a dark thought creeping into her mind. In that brief moment, Laura thought of only one possible suspect. "About a month ago, we had a teenager come to the clinic. He was upset about something his father had done."

"Go on."

Not wanting to divulge the particulars, she shook her head. "I can't talk about it—except that the teen was traumatized by what had happened. I counseled him, told him how to get help from the authorities next time it happened. He didn't want to report the incident, but I could tell he was afraid. He was a lot stronger and calmer after our first couple of sessions, though. Then he didn't come back."

"Did he seem angry at you?"

"No, he was angry at the world." And his father. The man had been extremely demanding and controlling. How could she tell Paco this without getting upset or giving away personal information? Or her acute sense of failure. "The young man killed himself about two weeks after he'd talked to me."

Paco scribbled some notes. "What was his name?"

"Is this necessary?"

"We have to assume, yes."

"Kyle Henner. He was sixteen."

She watched as Paco pulled up a number on his phone. "Kissie, it's Paco. Yeah, I'm okay. I need you to run a name for me. See what you can find out about a kid from Phoenix named Kyle Henner." He held the phone away. "Father's name?"

Laura hesitated then said, "Lawrence Henner. He's a big-time developer of some sort. He owns a lot of different companies. Lots of money and lots of power. He was devastated about what happened."

She didn't add that the man was also a walking time bomb who'd verbally abused not only his son but his wife, too. His wife left him after Kyle's suicide. And now that she thought about it, Lawrence Henner was just the kind of man to blame someone else for his son's death.

Someone like her, maybe?

Paco finished his conversation with Kissie then turned to Laura. "She'll get back to us. And if you think about anything else you can tell me about this kid, let me know."

"His father is ruthless," she said, her nerves sparkling with apprehension. "But I don't think he'd try to shoot me. He'd just find a way to ruin my life, probably."

"Or if he's that powerful, he could send someone else to shoot you."

She swallowed back her worries. "Last I heard, Mr. Henner had left the country."

"That could be a red flag."

"Or maybe he needed to get away from everything in the same way you did?"

He gave her a hard stare. "Maybe. Only I'm not the one out there in the hills with a gun, now, am I?"

Laura shivered at his words. No, he wasn't out there trying to shoot people. But if he didn't unload some of his own grief soon, he could be the next one.

How in the world could she help Paco Martinez deal with post-traumatic stress if someone was trying to finish her off before she even got started? That thought caused her to gasp and grab at Paco's hand.

"Did you remember something else?"

"No, but I just realized something."

His dark eyes swirled with questions. "Spit it out."

"What if that person out there was trying to *stop* me from talking to *you?*"

THREE

She had a point there. And she had already suggested he might be the target. But killing her for talking to him—or to keep her from talking to him—that was a different twist. Paco couldn't deny he had people gunning for him on so many levels. But to try and take out a pretty, innocent woman just because she was trying to help him. Who would want to do that? Maybe the shooter *had* been after *him* to begin with. That made more sense.

But he'd gone on a long run early this morning. It would have been easy for someone to spot him and take him out there in the desert. And by the time anybody found him, the vultures and other predators would have finished him off, anyway. No, this shooting had been timed for her arrival, by Paco's way of thinking.

"So maybe I should be asking you all these questions," she said, her expression bordering on smug. "I've read your case file. You've had quite a career in both special ops and with CHAIM. Both classified, of course, but I know things went bad on your last mission in Afghanistan. That's a lot of stress for any one man."

Paco wanted to laugh out loud, except a burning rage

kept him from cracking a smile. That and the way she'd changed from timid to tempest by turning the tables on him. "You have no idea, darlin'."

Her expression turned sympathetic, which only made things worse. He could handle anything but pity. "I think I do. That's why you called me that night."

He got up, stomping around the small café, his gaze hitting on an old shelf full of several carved wooden figurines of warriors astride horses his grandfather had created to sell right along refrigerator magnets, greasy hamburgers and ice-cold soft drinks. Grandfather Rainwater was content with his life.

Paco, however, was still struggling with his.

And this perky little counselor lady wasn't helping matters. Neither was being shot at so early in the day.

Remembering his midnight-hour shout-out, he said, "I shouldn't have called the hotline that night. False alarm."

"You called for a reason. Maybe someone else out there thinks you have a problem."

Paco turned to lean over the table, glad when she slid into the corner of the booth. Glad and a little ashamed that he'd stoop to a frowning intimidation to make her go away. "You wanna know why I called that night? Really want to know?" He didn't wait for her to nod. Pushing so close he could see the swirling violet-blue of her eyes, he said, "I wanted to take a drink. I wanted to get so drunk I could sleep for a week without nightmares or guilt or regret."

He lifted up and sank back down, the shock in her vivid eyes undoing him. "But I promised that old man in the kitchen back there that I was done with drunken brawls and feeling sorry for myself. I respect him and I didn't want to let him down. You see, he lost his son—in-law—my father—to the Vietnam War. And you probably know about my brother—he's in a wheelchair, compliments of Desert Storm. But…it's hard sometimes, in the middle of the night. So I wanted a drink, okay. But I didn't take that drink. Instead I prayed really hard and in a moment of sheer desperation, I dialed the number on the card Warwick gave me and blurted out all of my frustrations to you."

Hitting a finger hard on the table, he said, "I hope you're satisfied now. All clear?"

"Do you still want to drink?" she asked in a silky-strong whisper, her wide-eyed expression daring him to deny it.

Paco looked down at her, saw the strength pushing away the fear in her eyes, the solid concern out-maneuvering the shock on her face. He had to admire her spunk. His grandfather was the only person in the world who never backed down when it came to Paco and his moods.

Maybe he's finally met someone else worthy of that kind of status. Someone else he could learn to respect. And someone else who was willing to go the distance with him.

"Yes, I still want a drink," he said, surprised at this whole conversation. "But I won't take another one. I go to my AA meetings on a regular basis. I'm better now, I told you. So let's focus on the problem we have here, right now."

The doubtful stare she gave him implied she didn't believe him but she nodded her head in understanding. And right now, Paco couldn't worry about what she thought.

"Are you driving back to Phoenix today?" he asked, pulling her up out of the booth.

The confusion in her eyes slammed head-on into his own conflicting feelings. "No. I have a hotel room at the foot of the Grand Canyon." Looking sheepish, she said, "I thought if I couldn't find you I'd do a little hiking."

He drew in air, thinking it a blessing she'd found him. Just the thought of her alone near the Canyon with a lunatic tracking her sent fingers of dread racing across his spine. "Does anyone know where you are?"

"My parents and my supervisor at the clinic."

"Would they tell anyone else?"

"They might mention I'm at the Canyon. I didn't exactly post what I was doing. Just told them I'd be gone for a few days on a trip to locate a client."

A knock at the restaurant door caused Paco to spin around. His grandfather came out of the kitchen. "It's a delivery man bringing fresh produce," Walter said, waving Paco away. "Sorry. They usually pull around to the back."

Paco watched as Walter headed to open the door, the hair on the back of his neck bristling. His gaze hit Laura's, both of them realizing too late—

"Grandfather!"

Paco went into motion, rushing toward the door. But Walter already had it open, a smile on his face. "Joseph, why didn't you—"

A fist in Walter's face knocked the old man back onto the floor. Walter hit his head on the corner of a bench as he went down. Then he didn't move.

Paco heard Laura's scream even while he rushed the man at the door, taking the intruder by surprise, one hand pressing down on the man's weapon hand and the other one on his throat. With a grunt and heavy pressure on the wrist, Paco forced the man to drop the handgun he was carrying. But his opponent didn't let that stop him. He reached around with his other hand and tried to bring Paco down. Paco countered with an uppercut to the man's chin. Then they went down with fists popping against skin. The man was big and solid but Paco didn't let up until he had him rolled over faceup. Struggling to hold the man down, Paco memorized his face—scarred and brutal—just before he slammed his fist back into it.

Laura ran to Walter. "Mr. Rainwater? Are you all right?" Paco's grandfather didn't respond. Blood poured out of his nose and his breathing was shallow. Deciding the best thing she could do right now was to help Paco, she searched for a weapon and saw Walter's rifle leaning against the kitchen door. Without thinking, Laura grabbed it, trying to focus on the man who'd managed to get in and knock out Paco's grandfather. When Paco rolled the man over and begin hitting him in the face, she waited, her pulse flat-lining then spurting into overdrive. But the stranger reached up and managed to get his hands around Paco's neck. Paco grunted, working to flip the man over. When that didn't work, he tried hitting at the man again but he couldn't break away. Pushing at the man's thick arms, Paco finally managed to get his own fingers around the other man's throat.

Then it became a battle of wills as both held tight, each trying to squeeze the life out of the other. She had to do something. If she didn't stop this, Paco might not make it.

Laura raised the gun, her heart beating a prayer for

strength. And a prayer for good eyesight. She'd come across the state to save Paco, not watch him die. She would have to shoot the intruder.

Paco knew he wouldn't be able to hold out much longer. Matched in sheer strength by the other man, he fought for control—and his life. With each grunt, each surge of renewed energy, he wrestled and pushed his fingers against the stranger's thick throat muscles. If he could just find the right amount of pressure—

The room shook with a thundering roar and then the man holding Paco in a death grip went limp, his hands loosening and falling away, his expression going from determined and enraged to a surprised tranquility. Paco watched while the intruder's bulging, hate-filled eyes closed and he fell back on the floor with a heavy thud. For a minute, Paco didn't let go of his own frozen grip on the man's throat. But the silence and his own fast-moving breath brought him out of his stupor.

Looking up and around, he caught at a hitched breath. "Laura?"

She stood with the shotgun aimed high, her whole body trembling. "I'm okay."

Paco hopped up and stared down at the blood flowing from the stranger's side. The man wasn't breathing. Then he hurried to her. "Laura?"

"Your grandfather," she said, pointing a shaking hand toward the floor. "Go check on him!"

Paco took the gun, prying it away from her white-knuckled fingers to carefully lower it to a table. Then he went into action.

"Grandfather?" Paco felt for a pulse, relief washing through him when he found a faint beat pumping inside his grandfather's wrinkled neck. "Wíago, talk to me!" Turning Walter's head, he saw blood on the floor then felt around until he found the deep gash on the old man's skull. "He's bleeding from his nose and he hit his head. We need to get him to a doctor."

"I'll call 911."

Paco lifted up, torn between getting the dead man out of the way and taking care of his grandfather. He didn't have a choice. His grandfather could die. They had to call for help.

"I'll do it," he told Laura. Thinking about the implications of the scene, he said, "I'll have to explain this was self-defense." He pulled out his phone and dialed, telling the operator to hurry. "My grandfather was attacked by an intruder and when he fell, he hit his head. He's not responding. Yes, he has a pulse, but it's weak." He hurried to the man lying near the door and felt his pulse. "And the intruder is dead. Yes, from a gunshot wound. Can you please send someone?"

After giving the dispatcher their location, he brought a blanket from the small den in the back and wrapped it around his grandfather, then checked him over again to be sure there were no other injuries. After doing everything he could to make Walter comfortable, Paco left the dead man where he was—afraid to disturb the scene. Then he finally turned to Laura.

And saw that she was about to fall into a heap on the floor.

"Laura," he said, hurrying to her, wishing the nearest hospital wasn't so far away. "Laura, are you sure you're all right?"

She bobbed her head, her arms crossed around her

midsection, her gaze locked on the gruesome site of the man by the door. "Is that man dead?"

He pulled her close, leveling his gaze on her until she looked at him. "Yes, he is. You saved my life." He was as amazed by that as she seemed to be.

"I…I didn't know what to do. I had to stop him…and I thought I'd shot you at first. Is your grandfather going to be okay?"

With each word, tears brimmed in her eyes until one lone drop moved down her right cheek. Paco reached up and caught the tear, keeping his gaze locked on her. "I hope so. I think he's got a concussion and he'll need stitches for the gash on his head. I've made him comfortable and the paramedics are on the way. But it'll take them a few minutes. Let me check you over."

She tried to push away and stumbled, her face deadly pale. "I'm okay. I…Paco, I think I'm going to be sick."

Paco hurried her to the tiny bathroom in the back and waited at the door, keeping watch on his grandfather while he paced. When she came out a few minutes later, her skin was whitewashed with shock and she held a damp paper towel to her mouth.

"Better?" he asked, guiding her to a chair.

"I think so." She looked up at him, her eyes as blue as a desert sky at midnight. "I've never killed anyone before. Now I know how you must feel."

That statement punctured Paco's heart. How could such an innocent woman ever know or understand the way he felt? How could she be so brave, coming here to find him simply because she was worried about him? How could she get herself caught up in something that was probably of his making, put herself on the line like that for him, when she didn't even know him?

Before he could speak, she touched a trembling hand toward his heart. "I know what you were searching for that night, Paco."

Paco swallowed back the lump in his throat, the sound of distant sirens echoing inside his head right along with the rising echo of his pulse. She'd called him Paco. That meant she trusted him now, meant he'd allowed her to get that close already.

"What then?" he asked, unable to stay quiet, unable to comprehend this whole morning.

"You were looking for your heart. You wanted your soul back." She cleared her throat, her delicate hand warm on his chest, her gaze full of understanding and redemption. "I read a poem once where there was this heart hunter. He was searching for his own heart. He wanted to feel that warmth in his soul again. You know, that warmth that comes from faith and love and grace. And forgiveness. And so do you, I think. That's something we can all understand, something everyone longs for."

Paco lifted away, his head down. Grandfather always said there were no coincidences in life. He believed the Father knew all and saw all. Had God seen Paco's pain that night, the struggle for his soul, the struggle he'd battled through between the Bible he'd clutched and the bottle that was trying to clutch him, all night long and well into the early light?

Had God sent Laura to him?

"We have to get you out of here," he said in response, his thoughts too raw and fresh to express right now. He didn't know how to voice his thoughts, even on a good day. "They'll want a statement. Let me do all the talking. If they do ask you questions, just answer as briefly as possible. And be completely honest."

She dropped her hand away. "I have to tell them I shot that man."

Missing her warmth and needing to protect her, Paco said, "We could tell them I did it."

"No, I won't lie to them. And you said to be honest. I shot him because he was trying to kill you. That's the truth."

Paco knew she was right. They couldn't lie. But he had a very bad feeling about this whole situation. And he knew this wasn't over. Someone had sent a killer here two different times this morning. And they would keep coming until they hit their target.

He headed to the door to show the paramedics where to go and to greet the two officers pulling up outside. Then he glanced back at Laura to make sure she was holding up.

She gave him a wobbly half smile, her eyes still moist. Then she pushed at her hair and straightened her clothes, her head lifting as her eyes met his again.

And Paco had to wonder who in the world would want to hurt this woman?

She'd come here to help him, but in doing so she might have put herself in danger. Then she'd somehow managed to shoot a man in order to save Paco, which meant she was stronger than she looked. But that also meant she was now Paco's responsibility.

He had to get his grandfather to a safe place and he had to protect this woman no matter what. Maybe in the process, he just might find that heart she thought he was searching for.

Or lose it completely to the woman who'd come with such an unexpected determination into his life.

FOUR

Paco went into action after the ambulance and the sheriff's deputies left. Good thing the deputies knew his grandfather and him well enough to access the situation and keep it under wraps for now.

"I have to call my brother." Touching a finger to his phone, he waited, his eyes never leaving Laura. "Hey, Buddy. It's me, Paco. There's been a break-in at the café. Grandfather was hurt."

"Hurt? Is he okay?"

His brother's worried question filtered over the line. "He's unconscious. Got knocked on the head. Listen, they took him to the regional hospital near Jacob Lake. I have a situation here, so I need you to go to the hospital and call me with a report."

"What kind of situation?"

Paco huffed a breath. "I can't explain right now." Then he said on an urgent whisper, "I'm on the job."

His brother's silence told Paco Buddy was processing this. His older brother would understand and take action. "Can you talk?"

"Negative."

"Will you call me?"

"Yes. Just go to Wíago and stay with him. Call me

when you hear anything from the doctors. Or I'll call you when I get things straight here."

"Got it. I'm on my way to the hospital."

Paco turned toward Laura. "Let's get out of here."

"Where are we going?"

He didn't explain. He had enough to think about without having to report every detail to her. Seeing the distress in her eyes, he gently lifted her up. "You'll be okay. This has become official now."

She followed him without protest. Getting an argument from her would have eased Paco's mind even if he didn't want to hear it. She might be going into shock and that was the last thing he needed right now.

"Do you think the sheriff believed us?" she asked. "I mean, he didn't take me away. I thought he'd take me into custody after I told him what I'd witnessed and what happened." She didn't finish, didn't state the obvious.

Paco did a scan of the road and the desert, careful to shield her by keeping her behind him. "I explained things to the sheriff. Self-defense. He's a good friend of my grandfather's and for that reason he trusted me and he'll keep a lid on this for as long as possible. We both gave a statement and we've been cleared for travel."

"Cleared?"

He shoved her into his truck and closed the door. Once he was inside and feeling confident that they weren't being watched, he turned to her. "CHAIM clearance. For your safety, you're in my custody until we figure this out. The sheriff knows how to reach me if he needs to talk to us. We always alert the locals when we're on a case."

"Oh, of course."

Paco didn't like her quietness but he let it ride for now

while he watched the long, flat road and did a couple of quick searches of the desert on either side. When they turned off the dusty lane to his trailer, he slowed the truck.

"I live there," he explained, pointing to the tiny white home on wheels. "I need to get some equipment and then we're going to your hotel room to check it out."

"All right." She studied the travel trailer, her gaze moving between the RV and his face. "That's not very big."

"I don't need much space." Except the emotional kind, he thought, refusing to elaborate out loud.

She went silent again.

"Stay right here while I get some things," he told her. Then he handed her a loaded handgun he kept in the glove compartment, removing the safety before he handed it to her. "Use this if you have to."

Before she could protest, Paco was out the door and running toward the trailer.

Laura sat staring down at the gun. She's just shot and killed a man and now she was holding a gun. What had become of her life, of her plans to help Luke Martinez?

Paco.

The man frightened her as much as he intrigued her. He was all muscle and male, all mad and mysterious. Not the kind of man to whom she was attracted. No, she went more for the button-down, preppy type. But then, that type hadn't exactly been working out for her lately, come to think of it. Her last boyfriend hadn't taken their break-up very well. And why was she even thinking along those lines anyway? She'd come here on a mission of mercy, her faith intact, her concern real.

And now, in the span of less than two hours, she'd been shot at and she'd killed a man. And she still didn't understand who these people wanted to kill—her or Paco.

She looked out across the Painted Desert toward the mountains. They looked misty and solid as they hunched in watercolor shades of orange and mauve like sleeping giants off in the distance, the saguaros and fan palms stark and scattered across the arid vastness.

Who was out there?

Laura felt a chill in spite of the rising heat. She had to get out of this truck. She didn't want Luke to be alone. And she didn't want to be alone. They should stick together. She opened the door and hurried around to the back of the tiny trailer, her gaze taking in the canvas covered tented porch, a small grill and one lonely scarred lawn chair.

He didn't need much space.

Except the desolate emptiness of a desert.

What had she gotten herself into?

Paco whirled when he heard footfalls on the rickety steps, his gun trained on the door.

"I told you to stay in the truck," he shouted, relief washing over him. Relief followed by remorse. Laura was standing with one foot inside the door and the other one lowered on the steps, her gun shaking in her tiny hand.

"I was worried about you," she said, her gaze sweeping the cramped kitchen. Lowering the gun to the step, she asked, "Are you always this messy?"

"I didn't do this, sweetheart," he replied, disgust making him harsh as he looked over the ruin of his home. Someone had gone through ever nook and cranny, without regard for clothing, dishes or paperwork.

"Apparently, I had a visitor this morning." He touched a hand to something on the counter. "And they left yet another one of your business cards."

She stepped away. "What? But why?"

At least that shocked her out of her fear again. Good. She needed to clear her head because they were just getting started with this thing.

"Good question," he replied as he strapped on knives and guns, tugging weapons in his boots and underneath his shirt. "Either you have a fan, or someone is stalking you."

She looked up at him then, her eyes coloring to a deep blue. "Oh, no. No, it can't be."

She fell back and turned to sit on the metal step. Paco quickly slid out the door and hopped around her then turned to face her. "Talk to me, beautiful."

Laura put her head down in her hands. "I dated a guy for a few months, a while back. On the surface, he was a successful nice guy who said all the right things. But after a few months, things got weird and I broke it off. He started harassing me and I had to take out a restraining order. But he stopped bothering me about a month ago."

Paco leaned down, one hand reaching to lift her head up. "Define 'weird.'"

"After we broke up, he'd still call me and text me all day and night. He got really angry when I didn't call him right back. I got a funny feeling—instincts I guess. I told him to quit pestering me. He didn't take that very well. When he turned violent, I knew I'd made a big mistake. I think he suffered from paranoid delusional disorder."

"Did he hurt you? Hit you?"

She looked away. "He slapped me once."

Paco couldn't tolerate men who hit women. "And?"

"And I reminded him that we were over, he left a note on my apartment door, threatening me, calling me a tease." She looked up at Paco. "I never teased him or led him on about anything. I thought we were having a friendly relationship that might turn into something else. It didn't turn into anything but…creepy. I told him he needed help. I even offered to find him a therapist, since I certainly couldn't deal with him."

"You think this might be the guy?"

"I don't know. He stopped calling me after I took out the restraining order. I live in a secure building with a doorman, so everyone watched out for me. I would have known if he'd come back there."

"What's his name?"

She looked at the phone he'd pulled out of his pocket. "Alex Whitmyer. He came from a prominent family. He was handsome and a bit narcissistic, which I figured out a little too late. I'm still embarrassed about it. I'm supposed to help people like him, but I was too caught up in the relationship to see he was sick. And he was very good at hiding his real personality."

Paco wondered about that. Wasn't she supposed to be able to read people? Maybe not with her heart, but with her head. Had she cared about this guy? "I'll put in a call to Kissie. She can check him out in addition to the father of that kid you mentioned, too."

"Mr. Henner," she said, shaking her head. "I'd put

my money on Alex. He was just strange enough to go all ballistic and decide to teach me a lesson."

"But you didn't know our intruder. Why would he send other people to do the deed if he's the one stalking you?"

"He certainly could hire someone to scare me, but then so could Mr. Henner. Maybe it wasn't Alex after all."

He made the call to Kissie, giving her Alex Whitmyer's name. After explaining what had happened, he said, "Looks like I'm on a case, Kissie-girl."

"Paco, you sure you're ready for this?"

"Not you, too," he replied, closing his eyes. "I told Warwick I was doing okay."

"Well, he's so happy he just wants everyone else to feel the same," Kissie said through a chuckle. "Me, I think you find your strength when you need it the most."

"Well, then, we're about to test that theory," Paco replied. "Look, about Alex Whitmyer." He looked at the card. "He dated Laura Walton. Counselor. Works for CHAIM-approved clinic in Phoenix. Except right now, she's with me. I'm sure you've been updated on the shooting here this morning since I had to get clearance from both the sheriff and CHAIM to move the client."

"Heard all about it. We've got your back, Paco. And I've heard of Laura's work at the Phoenix Rising Counseling Center. But how in the world did she wind up with you?"

"She thinks I need counseling for some strange reason."

"I know Laura," Kissie said. "We've met at some of

the company get-togethers. Nice girl. And if anyone can help you, it'd be Laura. Do you need help?"

Paco grunted. "Why is everyone asking me that?"

"We care about you. What about the get-together at Eagle Rock. You gonna be there?"

"Hadn't planned on it," Paco replied. "Since when did CHAIM start having company functions anyway?"

"You've been out of the country too long, my child. We like to get together for some down time now and then. Good for the soul. And just FYI, this is a big to-do coming up next week at Eagle Rock. You know, to remember the fallen on Veteran's Day and to celebrate Thanksgiving. You should come. It's a mandatory callout."

"I'm kinda busy here, Kissie. We'll have to see about that."

"Okay then, but you might want to read the memo. I'll get right on this. You take care of my girl Laura, you hear."

"I hear."

He signed off then turned to Laura. "Kissie seems to think you're a nice girl."

"I am a nice girl," she replied without skipping a beat. "And I'm still wondering how I managed to kill a man."

He hated the tiny bit of little girl in her voice. She was way too nice to be sitting here in this old trailer, in the middle of the desert, with him of all people. She was the good girl who went to church and baked cookies for nursing home residents and planted petunias by the back door. The good girl who actually tried to help warped, scarred, tired souls.

He was the bad boy who shunned crowds, liked his

solitude and really never let anyone get too close. He was the loner, the soldier, the warrior who'd fought the good fight and yet, had somehow managed to lose both his soul and his sanity in doing so.

"How *did* you wind up here?" he asked her.

"I wanted to talk to you," she reminded him.

He lifted her up, grabbed the gun she'd laid on the step and pulled her toward the truck. "Well, honey, that's gonna have to wait. 'Cause whoever this is, they seem to be determined to either scare you or kill you. I just don't get why they keep leaving your cards everywhere like a trail. They obviously want us to find these cards."

She grabbed the tattered card out of his hand then gasped. "I didn't notice this before but this isn't my updated business card, Luke. This looks like my old set of cards. I had them changed about two weeks ago. I added my website on the new ones."

"Then where did these come from?"

"I threw them in the recycling bin at my apartment building."

He steadied her hand to stare at the card. "So someone went through that bin and found them. How many did you have left?"

"About twenty-five or so. A little box—almost empty."

"Just enough to spread the word."

"And what is the word?"

"That's the big question," he replied. "That's what we need to find out."

"Do we have to report this to the police?"

"Not yet," he said as he guided her to the truck. "We gave our report this morning about the break-in and the shooting. We might have to go in for more questioning once they identify the man who—"

"The man I killed," she replied, her eyes going all misty. She turned away to stare out into the desert.

Paco didn't press her. Sooner or later, she was going to fall apart and they both knew it. He dreaded it. He'd never been good around hysterical women. But this one was deserving of a little meltdown. He'd see her through it, because *he* wasn't allowed to have any more meltdowns. He had a mission. And he was alone in this until he could figure out what was going on. He couldn't abandon this innocent woman even if he did resent her being here.

"Let's go," he said, tugging her toward the truck.

She wiped her eyes and got in, the big truck making her look even more lost and tiny. Which only made Paco want to protect her even more.

He slipped behind the wheel, shaking his head as he brought the truck to life with a roar. This day had gone from bad to worse. And he had a feeling it wasn't going to get any better anytime soon. His grandfather was in the hospital, probably still in a coma. His brother would want answers. Paco wanted those same answers.

After calling his brother one more time to check on his grandfather, Paco glanced over at the woman huddled in the seat across from him and wondered if he could keep her safe and alive until he figured things out. He had to. He wouldn't lose her. He wouldn't be the last man standing again.

Not this time. Not with Laura Walton. She deserved better than that. Much better.

FIVE

They drove the twenty miles to her hotel near the foot of the South Rim of the Grand Canyon. By now it was midday and a lot warmer in spite of the late fall temperatures. Laura's shirt was sticking to her back, chilling her as she cooled down.

Over the whirl of the faint air-conditioning in the old truck, Paco said, "Here's what we're gonna do. We'll check you out of the hotel and find a safe place to stay for tonight. That way, if you were tracked to the hotel, they'll know you're gone. Or if they've been there, we might find some kind of lead."

"Do you think someone already knows I'm staying there?" she said, glancing up at the stone front of the lobby entrance. This hotel had looked so serene when she'd arrived yesterday afternoon.

"Probably. And they probably couldn't find a way to get to you before you left this morning. Or they wanted to get you in an isolated situation."

"Which they did."

"Yes. Two attempted hits in as many hours so I can almost guarantee more will follow."

"I don't know why I'm a target," she said, grabbing the door handle. "I wish I could explain this."

He held tightly to the steering wheel, his silence stretching like the long road they'd just traveled. "You might be right about it being aimed toward me. Maybe someone didn't want you to talk to me for a reason."

"Or maybe they wanted to kill both of us for a reason."

"That's what we need to find out," he said as they left the truck and entered the hotel the back way. "Let's check out your room, see if anything looks suspicious."

"What if they're waiting for me?"

"I'll take care of that." He walked her up the empty hallway without making a sound. "Just stay behind me."

Laura wouldn't argue with that. He had a way of going noiseless in and out of places. But then, he was trained to be invisible. Right now, however, he was a very visible presence in her life. And a blessed one, considering she knew nothing about espionage or spying or killing people. She only knew how to help those who did so try and pick up the pieces when things got to be too much.

Was Luke ready to go back into the fray?

Please, Lord, let him be ready. Not for my sake but for his. She had a gut feeling if he failed this time, it would put him over the edge. She also had a feeling he hadn't talked to anyone much since he'd come home from the front. Shane Warwick had warned her Luke Martinez could be as quiet and stone-faced as a rock when he went into one of his dark moods.

She'd come here on a mission of her own, though. And she'd brought trouble to an already troubled man. So she prayed for guidance and mercy and protection for both of them. She wouldn't abandon him now, no matter the danger.

But when Luke opened her hotel room door and she saw what someone had done to her room, Laura knew this was about more than a jilted boyfriend stalking her or a grieving father seeking revenge. The bedspread and pillows were tossed and scattered, the drawers and closets thrown open and her clothes strewn around the room.

And her laptop was missing.

"I didn't bring it with me this morning," she said. "I had my phone and I'd downloaded your file onto it. I didn't bring the laptop in case I had to do some hiking. I thought it would be safer here than in the car." She turned to Paco, grabbing his hand. "They have my files. Everything is on that laptop."

"Explain *everything*."

"Notes on my patients, my personal files, you name it. My life is on there." She didn't tell him that she'd saved some personal information about him on there, too. "It's all encrypted and backed up on an external hard drive at my office, and I have a password, but still—"

Paco dropped his hands to his hips as he surveyed the damaged room. "And the hits just keep on coming. A password won't stop anyone if they want to get to your files, sweetheart." He gripped her shoulders. "Why would they take your laptop, Laura?"

She stared up at him, her mind racing with confusion. Then she straightened back into business mode. "Maybe they need information on one of my patients? Something damaging? But why would they want to kill me to get that?"

"Well, so you'd be out of the way. Which means this

information must be a big deal. Would your stalker guy want any of your files?"

"He might try to use them against me," she said. "I was a mess when Kyle committed suicide and I confided in Alex, without giving out any names."

Paco shook his head. "Doesn't add up. A stalker wouldn't try to kill you without confronting you. He'd want to justify his actions, try to reason with you. But he'd take you somewhere isolated so he could make you listen. And he wouldn't take your private files unless they had something to do with him."

"Do you think it could be Kyle's father then?"

"Could be. Maybe he wants to keep his son's illness and the counseling sessions a secret. But if he killed you, that would only open up a whole new can of worms. Again, doesn't make sense."

"None of this makes sense," she said. "No matter though, I'll have to answer to my supervisors about this. I might even lose my job." She looked down. "Just one more thing."

"You got something else on your mind, something you forgot to tell me?"

Laura didn't have a chance to respond. They heard footsteps in the hallway, causing him to quickly shut the door, lock it, then shoved her into a corner. "Whatever happens, you listen to me, you understand?"

She bobbed her head. "What if something happens to you?"

"Then you go out onto the balcony and jump, run and don't look back."

Laura prayed she wouldn't have to use that plan. Her room was on the fourth floor and she was deathly afraid of heights. She'd been to the Grand Canyon lots of times.

But she'd never once stepped close to the edge.

Paco pulled his handgun out of the holster and held it toward the door. Someone jingled the handle, once, twice. They'd have to either use a card key or break the door down. And if they did either, he'd be waiting for them.

"Maid service," came a feminine call. "Hello?"

He went to the door. "Come back later."

Waiting with the gun drawn, he listened then heard a cart rolling away.

"Was that really the maid?" Laura asked from her corner.

"Can't say, not knowing," he replied. "Let's get out of here." When she rushed for the door, he snagged her arm. "Not that way. We leave by the balcony."

Laura stepped back, shaking her head. Then she started tidying the place, shutting drawers, fluffing pillows. "Isn't there another way?"

Paco counted to ten, taking in her sudden burst of nervous energy. The woman was intelligent so what was she missing here. He pointed to the door. "There is that way where someone could be waiting to ambush us, or there is the balcony—the quickest way to escape."

She straightened the ice bucket, setting it straight. "I vote the stairs."

"Bad choice. Too isolated and too easy for someone to be lurking about. So I vote the balcony." His patience wearing thin, he asked, "Just what is the problem here, Laura?"

She shifted, fidgeted, looked away. "I... I don't like high places."

He frowned, lifting his eyebrows. "Say that again?"

"I don't do high places. I'm afraid of heights, okay?"

"But you're at the Grand Canyon!"

"Yes, but I didn't come to see the canyon. I came to find you."

Putting a finger to his forehead, Paco said, "But you said you planned to do some hiking if you failed at finding me."

"Yes," she said on a frustrated whisper. "Low hiking. As in at the bottom of the canyon or maybe in some part of the canyon but not near the very edge of the high-up canyon."

Tugging her toward the balcony door, he said, "This is only a few floors up, sweetheart. And it's grassy down there. It won't hurt a bit."

"I can't do it." She held back, a solid fear centered in her eyes. "My office is on the second floor of the clinic and my apartment in Phoenix is on the first floor. I usually don't go above level three but this was the only room available. I don't like elevators, either."

"Well, then we're in serious trouble. We can't take the stairs or the elevator here. The only way out is through that balcony door and down."

She ventured a glance out the door. "But we can't just jump."

"I can. And I'm pretty sure you'll be able, too. Since it might mean saving your life."

"But what if they're down there waiting?"

A good point. Paco pushed her away from the door. "I'll check things out." Slowly opening the sliding glass door, he peaked out and looked both ways then glanced down at the parking lot. "I don't see anyone but anything is possible." Then he turned back to her. "I think I see a way to do this."

"What?"

The wash of pure relief in her eyes told him she was serious about being afraid of heights. Another thing he'd have to remember right along with finding out what else she might be hiding from him.

"We can move from balcony to balcony until we reach the outside stairs at the end of the building. Do you think you can deal with that, at least?"

She walked to the open door and peered at the wide wooden-planked balconies. Then she took in a long breath. "I'll try."

Paco heard footsteps out in the hallway. "Good, because I think our visitors are back. And this time I don't think they're concerned about housekeeping."

Before she could panic, he shoved her and her big purse out the door and slid it shut. Holding her away from the open banisters, he said, "Don't think about it. Just act. That's how you survive sticky situations. You just have to take action."

She bobbed her head, her eyes glazing with fear. "I'll try, Paco. I promise."

Good grief, did she have to go all girly on him now? The woman had faced down an intruder and shot him dead. He needed her to stay strong until he could find a safe place to stash her.

"Okay, let's do it then. I'm going to climb over first," he said, dragging her stiff form along. "Then I'll help you over. We do that until we reach the end, okay?"

She strapped her bag across her body as if it were a shield. "Okay."

It was a weak "okay" but he'd have to go with it. "Don't think about it and don't look down. Just focus on getting from balcony to balcony."

She nodded again, her eyes so big and blue he had to look away—or he'd chicken out too just to spare her—and that would be bad for both of them.

He leapt over the first sturdy railing then turned to take her hand. "That's it. I've got you. Just about a half foot between them. Plenty of room."

She scooted across, holding on to him for dear life until he had her over the railing and on solid flooring again, her shoulder bag slung across her body and swinging out as he lifted her.

"See, not so bad. Just three more to go."

"It looks like a lot more to me."

"Just three—then we'll take the outside stairs and be on our way."

If they didn't get assaulted at the corner of the building. He'd have to do a thorough overview before they could advance toward the parking lot and his truck.

"Here we go," he said as he pulled her over the second railing. Glancing inside the room, he noticed an old woman standing there in a jogging suit drinking coffee. Paco waved and kept going. He didn't have time for explanations.

"The last one, Laura," he said, not used to having to be so nice when giving commands or instructions. It was as foreign to him as holding her hand. Especially since she'd come charging into his safe, secure, quiet world and brought his heart right out its flat-lining existence.

Holding her hand, however, was one thing. Keeping her alive was a whole different thing.

"Last one. See, that wasn't as hard as you thought."

She didn't answer. But when he tugged her over the last balcony and settled her on the landing near the hallway door to the inside of the building, she held to his arms with an iron grip. Surprising since she didn't seem to weigh much more than a doll.

"Laura?"

She wasn't listening. Instead, she was staring off over his shoulder. Great. Had she gone into shock again? Or was she about to have that meltdown he'd been dreading.

"Laura, we need to keep moving?"

"Paco," she whispered, her voice low and tight-edged. Then she pointed. "Look at your truck."

He whirled, gun lifting, his gaze moving across the big parking lot. Then with a grunt he dropped his gun down by his side and stomped a boot against the wall. "They slashed my tires!"

"That means they've been watching us. And now we can't leave." She moved near him with an almost automatic need, as if she knew he was her protector now, whether she liked it or not. And whether he wanted to be or not. "What do we do now?"

He let out a breath of pure aggravation then pulled her back against the wall while he scanned the empty parking lot. "Well, beautiful, you did say you wanted to do some hiking. I'd say now's your chance."

SIX

"My other hiking boots are in my car back at the café."

Paco eased her down the stairs, sticking to the wall while he scoped the parking lot. "Your car is no longer at the café. I had someone tow it away—to a safe place."

"Oh." She'd have to remember that this man was trained to be one step ahead of everything and everyone. Including her. "Thanks, I think."

He looked down at her low heeled sturdy boots. "Those should work. You might have to run, though."

"Since I've been shot at and chased already, I can do that," Laura replied, praying she could survive this. "Don't worry about me."

He huffed a chuckle. "Good one."

"Okay, worry about me then. What's the plan?"

"For now, to get around this wall and make sure the parking lot is secure."

Laura didn't push for more. He needed to focus and she wouldn't distract him. She knew this from her years working with CHAIM. She needed to clear her head, too. She'd come here on one quest but now things had changed into a full-fledged CHAIM mission. Now, she was running for her life with the very man she'd come to save.

Funny how the tables had turned on her. Maybe God was giving her a test. She'd been blessed with a good life and two loving parents, siblings to nag her and comfort her. Laura had never been through any kind of test such as this. She'd breezed through school and college, hired on with CHAIM right away and found work at a good clinic in Phoenix. A charmed life, some would say. A blessed life for sure.

Then two things had happened. She'd broken up with Alex not long after Kyle had ended his life, forcing her to wonder what she could have done differently in both situations. She wanted things to be different for Paco. She wanted to help him, had come here to validate her professional skills.

But someone out there had a bone to pick with her. Someone out there wanted her dead. The chill of that ran down her spine with all the pressure of bony fingers. But the injustice of it made her spine stiffen.

She instinctively clung to Paco's shirt but vowed to get herself out of this fix, somehow.

"Looks clear," he said on a low whisper. "We're going to head for those trees to the right. That should give us enough shelter to get us out on the road and away. We can hide behind buildings as we go." He turned, bumping into her, his big body blocking her fears about the outside world, but opening up a whole new set of conflicting emotions inside her heart.

"Stay behind me and hold on to my shirt. If I tell you to run, let go and run behind me, okay? But keep me in your sights."

"Okay."

"On the count of three." Paco counted then took off in a running crouch, his gun drawn. Laura held to his shirt, leaning low as they hurried across the open parking lot.

They made it into the trees then he whirled to tug her behind him while he scanned the area. "So far, so good. Must still be in the building looking for us." Turning to check on her, he said, "Next plan of action—try to find a way out of here."

"We're not going up into the canyon, are we?"

"No. We don't want to get in a ruckus that might injure tourists or attract the park rangers. Not so hot. The idea is to draw our attacker away from this area. He wants to isolate us, but that can work to our advantage."

"But where will we go?"

He rubbed a hand across his brow. "My plan is to either get you back to Phoenix or to get you to Eagle Rock."

"Eagle Rock? That's in Texas."

"Yes, but it's our main safe house. The security is so tight you'd have to bring in an army to get to anyone staying there. Warwick helped update everything recently, since we're all supposed to convene there for some sort of retreat next week. I hadn't planned on attending but maybe that's the best place for you, so I guess we're going to the party."

"You have to attend anyway," she said. "It's mandatory."

"Yeah, only CHAIM would suggest a retreat then make it mandatory. I don't do mandatory very well."

"But if you take me there—"

"I'll have to sign up for the fun stuff. I get that."

That he was willing to do that for her spoke volumes

about Paco Martinez. In spite of his tough, gruff exterior he was redeemable. But then, she had believed that since the night she'd heard his voice rasping across the phone line. She'd hold to that belief until they could get past this threat.

"Thank you," she said, determined to stick with him no matter what.

"My job," he replied, obviously just as determined to finish this and get her off his back. He glanced around one more time. "This is a busy area. I don't think they'd try anything but then, they did mess up my truck and trash your room."

"They have my laptop now. Maybe that's all they wanted."

"Maybe. Maybe not. Let's get moving."

He checked his phone. "Hold on. I've got a message from my brother." He pulled up the number and waited. "Buddy, talk to me."

Laura listened as he repeated to her what his brother was saying.

"Wíago's still in a coma. They're doing tests." He waited then said, "But he's in good physical shape." He looked into Laura's eyes. "Something about bleeding in the brain or swelling."

Laura digested the information. "Bleeding in the brain—a hematoma. That means they might have to do surgery to relieve the pressure."

Paco nodded, repeating what she'd said back to his brother. "Yeah, exactly." He looked at her. "Buddy says that's pretty much what the doctor told him." Then he talked to his brother a couple more minutes. "We're safe for now. No, you stay with Grandfather. The sheriff is investigating the guy who broke into the café. I'll be in touch."

Laura watched as he hung up. "I'm sorry. It sounds as if your grandfather's injury has gone from a concussion to brain trauma. That's serious, Luke."

He looked out over the trees. "Tell me something I don't know."

Laura gulped, thinking one of his black moods was coming. Guilt weighed at her, dragging her down. If she'd stayed in Phoenix, this wouldn't have happened. But then, if she hadn't come here, would someone have come after her in Phoenix? Or worse, come after Paco and killed him? Or did this person want them both dead? Her head hurt from tension and fatigue and shock. She'd like some answers, not constant questions inside her brain. But right now, she'd like to get away from the danger she felt pressing like a heavy fog all around them.

He dragged her along while she mulled over all the variables. Then he stopped so quickly, Laura plowed right into his broad back.

Paco turned to capture her in a long stare. "I don't get the card stuff. Why would they leave your card when they're obviously after *you?*"

"I don't know," she said, gulping back her intimidation. "Disturbed people aren't logical about certain things. They can justify any action with what they think is a good reason. Maybe leaving my card is a way of teasing me, letting me know they can find things that belong to me, even in a Dumpster. It's a tactic to scare me. Which it has, by the way."

Pulling her underneath the eaves of a tourist shop, Paco took out the two cards he'd saved, looking them over. He squinted then held one of the cards closer. "It looks like a watermark or something on the back of both cards."

Laura looked then pulled out her glasses from her purse pocket. "Maybe. Or it could be that they wrote something on a piece of paper that was pressed against the cards—some sort of cryptic message."

"A message to you?"

"Possibly. But why wouldn't they just write it out?"

"Like you said, sweetheart, disturbed people do strange things. And whoever this is must have some sort of plan that he's put into action. Starting with you and me."

He did a visual of the street. "Let's duck into the restaurant on the corner so I can check in. Kissie might be able to give me an update on the two names we sent her."

Aggravated and tired, she followed him. "Shouldn't we stay on the move?"

"We will after I decide where to move to next."

"Do we really have to leave Arizona?"

"Might be best." He nodded then followed the waitress to a booth in the corner. Pulling Laura in beside him, he whispered, "Let's sit together, facing the door."

Laura breathed in the scent of aftershave and sweat, her head reeling with thoughts and feelings best left unexplored right now. Paco practically filled the whole booth with his presence but she did feel safe all tucked in—or rather trapped—between him and the wall.

After they'd ordered sandwiches and coffee, he leaned so close she could see the rich brown around his almost black irises. "We're getting out of here. I have to arrange a few things first. We have a saying in the desert: 'Before you get somewhere, you have to go through a whole lot of nowhere.'"

"Are we going through the desert?"

"If we have to. The desert can hide a person for days."

Laura didn't relish that idea. While she was in pretty good shape, making a trek through the hot, dusty desert wasn't on her list of things to do while she was being chased by bad guys. Nor did she want to spend the night out in the barren hills.

He must have sensed her hesitation. "I know my way around, so don't worry."

"Right. I won't worry—not one little bit. Just like you won't worry about me—not at all. Good one."

"Okay, I get it." He shook his head then got Kissie on the phone. "What do you know?"

While he listened to Kissie's report, Laura kept her eyes on the door of the restaurant. Several other diners were settled into their meals and she sure didn't want anyone else to get hurt on her behalf. Praying that these people would leave them alone now that they had her laptop, she did a mental list of things to do.

Call her assistant to report the laptop missing.

Try to get her hard copy files moved to a safe location.

Have someone check her apartment—not a friend but someone official.

Try to stay alive until this was over.

She didn't realize he'd hung up the phone until she felt his hand touching her arm. "I've got some interesting news."

"What?"

"Kissie says Lawrence Henner has several homes

around the world. One in the Cayman Islands, an apartment in New York and...a lake house near Austin, Texas."

"Texas? Why? He can hunt and fish in Arizona."

"Bingo. Why would a man who has everything he needs here in Arizona need a lake house in Texas."

"Maybe he has relatives there. Or maybe he wanted a change of scenery—less desert and canyons and mountains."

"Or maybe he has business there. Business he doesn't want us to know about." He inhaled then added, "Nothing on your stalker boyfriend yet. And that right there should give us pause. He must be keeping a low profile these days."

A shudder of apprehension shimmied down her body. "So what do we do next?"

He was already hitting his apps. "First, I'll let my team know about this. They've been updated on what happened to us today, so they're already on high alert. We've sent people to report to your clinic about your laptop being stolen and we've checked out your apartment. It's been trashed. No surprise there."

Laura's heartbeat increased with each task. He'd just ticked off her to-do list. "I guess you moved my hard copy files to a secure location."

"Yeah, of course we did."

She felt better about the staying alive thing now. And wondered how he'd managed all of that when she'd never noticed him on the phone talking or texting. Well, maybe a couple of times during their drive here. Obviously the man was good at multitasking. "Thank you."

"Quit thanking me." He shrugged. "I don't know what it is, but something isn't right about this whole thing."

A lot wasn't right about this whole thing, Laura thought as she listened while he gave Shane Warwick all the details of this bizarre case. "Since you're in Texas now," he told Shane, "maybe you can do some recon work on this. And keep checking on Alex Whitmyer. I don't like the sound of him, either."

Apparently Shane agreed to that. Paco hung up just as the waitress brought their food. Then he ate his sandwich as if he were starving.

While Laura sat there breaking her food into tiny pieces. Her nerves were rattling and hitting against her insides so furiously, she felt as if she'd been on a roller coaster.

"Eat," he said, a firm tone stiffening his words. "You'll need your strength."

"Pray," she retorted, frustration coloring her suggestion. "*You'll* need your strength."

"Touché," he retorted. "But me and God, we're not talking much these days."

"But you said you prayed to Him."

"Oh, I do. But I'm not sure He's hearing me clearly."

"He listens. You made it through that rough night when you called me."

He took a drink of coffee then sat his cup down. "I believe the Father always listens. But I also believe that sometimes we're just not worth the fuss."

"You mean you think *you're* not worth the fuss. Luke, you have to know God won't abandon you."

He gave her a hard look. "He wasn't there the day my entire unit was mowed down on that mountain."

Laura had to change his perspective. "You lived for a reason, Luke."

"Oh, yeah. And what is that reason?"

She looked down at her cold food, took a deep breath and looked back up. "Me?" she asked on a squeaky voice. "Maybe I'm the reason you survived. Maybe God knew *I'd* need you one day."

SEVEN

His heart actually started beating faster.

Paco didn't know what to say to that. What did a man say to a woman who looked at him with big dark blue eyes filled to the brim with hope? What did a man who'd up until today been content to be completely alone say to a woman who made all of his protective instincts go into overdrive? A woman who made him think about nice things such as long walks and laughing out loud. Happiness. He didn't even know what happiness meant anymore. And he sure didn't know what God was all about anymore.

"Let's leave God out of this."

She looked disappointed and hurt. She turned away to stare out the window, her fingers twisting a paper napkin against the table. "We need Him now, Paco. I mean, really need Him."

Thinking he was truly lower than a snake's belly, Paco grabbed her hand. "I shouldn't have said that."

Laura glanced down at his hand over hers. "You have a lot of scars. God can heal them."

She was looking at the jagged white scars lining his knuckles. "Yes, I do. Some of them show and some of them don't."

That brought her gaze back up to him. "God can heal all of them. That's why I came to find you. I couldn't stop thinking about that night when you called. I wanted you to know that I can help you, too. That's why God called me to this career, I think. I always wanted to help other Christians, but I'm too chicken to go out into the missionary field or to do the type of things you do. My calling is in counseling and therapy. And I just knew God wanted me to find you. Especially after…"

"After what?" Did she have her own torment? He didn't have the right to ask her about anything. But between the abusive boyfriend and that kid's suicide, she probably had her own guilt weighing her down.

"Never mind," she said. "I came here all self-righteous and determined, wanting to make a difference in your life." She pulled her hand away. "But look at how that turned out. Running for our lives, getting shot at and shooting people." Her words became choppy with emotion. "Your grandfather—"

"Hey, Wíago is tough. He's been through worse. And my brother Buddy is right there with him, guarding him and watching over him. If it makes you feel better, Buddy knows how to pray. He has a pipeline right to God's ear."

She wiped at her eyes. "We all need to pray, for your grandfather, for whoever is doing this to us, for everything."

"Why don't you pray and I'll plan?"

She pushed her food away. "I'd feel better if we prayed together."

"Here, now?"

She bobbed her head, her eyes full of that glorious hope again.

"I... I'm not good at public displays of praying, Laura. I do my best bargaining with God when I'm faced with a bottle at three o'clock in the morning."

Her eyes widened then and he saw her go from sweet to steely. "Don't you see, Paco? That bottle of liquor represents all your torment and your shame and guilt. All the more reason to learn how to pray without ceasing, no matter the time of day."

"Got it." He looked around, uncomfortable with this whole conversation and stunned by her sharp-edged logic. It wasn't like they didn't have pressing matters to take care of—such as staying alive. But hey, he'd tried everything else. Pray might be their best option right now.

She must have sensed his near-compliance. "Here, take my hand and just close your eyes. Nobody is looking. And so what if they are?"

Paco grunted, but he took her tiny hand, his scarred fingers accepting the lace-delicate touch of her skin.

"Dear Father," she began, her voice going from strained to sure, "we don't know what's going on with us or why we are under siege. We do know that someone wants to do us harm. We ask that You intercede in this warfare, that You show us the right way and guide us through each step we take. And Lord, please help to change our pursuers—whatever their motives. Bless and keep Luke and Wíago and Buddy close, Lord. Protect them and guide them. Amen."

Paco kept her hand when she tried to let go. "Father, don't forget Laura."

When he opened his eyes, she has such a sweet, serene smile on her face Paco knew he was in serious trouble. His heart, so long guarded and lifeless, was pumping new blood through his veins with such intensity, he had to catch his breath.

To waylay that, he said, "Satisfied? We need to get moving."

She didn't answer, and if her smile seemed to fade at his callus treatment, he ignored it. He had to keep his emotions at bay so he could keep her alive.

That was *his* most urgent prayer right now.

Two hours later, they'd hiked out of the tourist-laden foot of the South Rim and were on some dusty back road into the desert. Laura was tired but secure in the knowledge that if anyone could get her across a desert, it would be Paco Martinez. He'd loaded up on gear after taking a quick shopping trip at one of the souvenir stores. He was now fortified with a backpack full of bottled water and power bars slung on his back along with the weapons of various shapes and sizes that's he'd strapped to his body earlier when they'd gone by his trailer, including a nasty-looking knife and a tiny pistol tucked inside his boot. He had compasses and maps and his trusty phone. And he'd made her buy a pair of sturdy hiking boots and good socks, using most of her cash.

While she felt safe knowing he was prepared, Laura also fretted about how he'd react to whatever came at them next.

Luke Paco Martinez was in full black ops mode from what she could tell. And that "take no prisoners" scowl he wore as they marched through the fall heat didn't bode well for anyone who crossed him. Including her.

"Rest," he said now, his tone curt and no-nonsense. He was the point man, of course, explaining that they would take a five minute rest at the top of every hour.

That five-minutes wasn't nearly enough for Laura but she didn't complain. She was at the man's mercy, after all.

He pointed to a big bronzed rock jutting out from a heavy cluster of yucca plants. Laura gingerly looked around for scorpions, snakes and spiders before she sank down on the warm rock.

"Drink." He handed her a bottle of water.

Laura took it and chugged until the bottle was unceremoniously taken out of her hands.

"Slow, sweetheart. Drink it slow."

Well, at least he was still calling her sweetheart. That endearment coming from any other man would have made her bristle. But Luke seemed to use it almost absent-mindedly, making her think he called a lot of people that.

Not just Laura Walton, and not because she was special. She was nobody special, just the woman he was now forced to protect. The woman who'd come here hoping to redeem herself away from the guilt nagging at her, hoping to cure her own ills and insecurities by picking Paco's brain. Fat chance of that. He'd have her talking and confessing everything from stealing a kiss from a boy in the fourth grade to eating too much ice cream while she watched sappy movies, she guessed, before he spoke to her of any of his own pain.

"Thanks," she said, handing the bottle back to him. "I'll save the rest for later."

He drank the rest. Then he halved a power bar and handed her part of it. "Eat."

Laura ate the chewy, nasty-tasting bar with a firm smile on her face.

His next words were, "Let's go."

"Could I ask where we're going?"

"To my brother's house. We can rest there and regroup."

"How far?"

"Another ten miles."

That sounded like a hundred miles in desert time, she decided. Hadn't they already been at least twenty miles? And because she needed to distract herself from the dry heat and the sun and the creepy-crawly things, she said, "I wish I knew why they wanted my laptop."

"To get information," he replied with a "duh" tone.

"But what information? How could they benefit from my patient files?"

"Maybe they wanted your personal stuff."

"That doesn't make any sense either. They apparently know a lot about me already." She shrugged. "And besides, I don't have much personal stuff. My work is my life." A sad admission and one she wished she'd kept to herself.

"Maybe they wanted to get next to you—that thing you said about showing you they could invade your privacy anywhere."

"That worked, then."

Laura decided she'd keep quiet for a while. He didn't seem in a chatty mood and she'd spill even more of her pathetic personal information if she didn't shut up.

Then out of the blue, he said "Tell me more about the stalker."

"Alex?" Surprise and dread filled her. "Big mistake. We met at a business function. He worked selling alarm systems and seemed to enjoy it. At first, he was so great—kind, considerate, fun to talk to. He asked me a lot of questions."

"Hold it right there. What kind of questions?"

"You know, about my life, my work. The usual."

"Sometimes the usual can be the most obvious."

"You mean, he had an agenda maybe?"

His grunt indicated yes. "How long did you date?"

"A few months. But then he got a little too possessive for me to feel comfortable. He became demanding and paranoid. He even accused me of cheating on him. Things escalated and I got scared. I tried to reason with him, tell him it just wasn't working. I offered to get him help. But he kept at me, telling me he loved me and we were made for each other. After he started showing up at my apartment and my work and sending constant text messages and voice mails, I broke things off. He cornered me in the parking lot and that's the day he slapped me. I was advised to take out a restraining order."

"And he didn't take that too well?"

"No. Not at all. His pleas turned to even more threats. But I never could prove much beyond the text messages I'd saved. He was always careful to leave typed notes or things that couldn't be traced. Little clues—"

She stopped. "Luke, little clues. What if this *is* him doing all of these horrible things and that's what he's done with my old business cards? Left some sort of clues or threats for me to find—just to scare me."

"Already considered that, sweetheart. I'm going to check those out more when we get to Buddy's place."

Well, of course he'd considered that. "Do you believe it's him then?"

He guided her past a giant saguaro. "I'm liking him for it, yeah. But it's almost too easy."

"Too obvious?"

"Yeah. Like I said, things don't add up. If he's stalking

you because he's obsessed with you, he wouldn't try to kill you right away. He'd want to come after you and maybe take you away to convince you to love him the way he loves you. And then he'd kill you if you didn't see things his way."

Laura shivered in spite of the rising heat. "If he was trying to do that, then he might have tried to shoot you, too. If he thought, you know, that you and I—"

"Possibly. But why send another hit man?"

"To keep his hands clean? Or to help him, make it easy for him to take me."

He shrugged, but the look he gave her reassured her. "If we ever get to a safe place, I'll sit down and figure this out." He turned, doing one of his panoramic views, looking behind them.

Laura turned to respond and found herself flat on the sandy desert floor, his hand over her head.

"Don't move," he said, drawing weapons with a swift clarity. "We have company."

Dirt ground like shards of glass against her skin. "Where?"

"On the road behind us to the east. Don't look."

Laura breathed dust, her pulse hitting against the hard desert floor, her mind very much aware of Paco there beside her. "How many?"

"Only one so far. I think I can take him."

She chanced a glance at him and watched as he pulled that mean-looking knife out of his boot. Not wanting to see this, Laura closed her eyes again and prayed with all her might.

Paco held his hand on her neck. "Don't move a muscle. We wait until he's right on us."

"Are you sure it's someone after us?"

"Yeah, since he's packing a high-powered rifle and since I'm pretty sure he has that rifle trained on the spot where he last saw us."

Beads of sweat caught in the center of her back between her shoulder blades and evaporated with each beat of her heart. Her throat was so dry, she couldn't force a swallow. Breathing became impossible. Then she lifted her head an inch and saw something that terrified her every bit as much as the person tracking them.

"Luke?"

"Shh."

"But—"

"Be still. I mean it."

She was going to pass out. Laura knew this but she couldn't voice it. She froze, her gaze fixed, her mind whirling with visions of imminent death.

"Luke, please?"

Had she managed to say that out loud?

She would never know because a gunshot rang out and then in one blur of motion she only caught out of the corner of her eye, she watched as Paco stood and threw the knife at their pursuer, hitting him square in the chest.

And then he whirled and shot in midair the rattlesnake rising up to strike just inches away from Laura's face.

EIGHT

"Are you hurt?"

Paco grabbed Laura, dragging her up with one arm, his gun still aimed on the twitching snake.

"I'm… I'm all right," she said. She buried her head against his chest and closed her eyes. "Is he dead?"

"The snake or the man?"

"Both?"

"Man down and snake giving his last dying twitch. You can open your eyes now."

She lifted away to stare up at him. "I can't take much more of this. I thought snakes went into hibernation this time of year." But obviously, bad guys didn't.

He glanced at the dead snake. "That old-timer was probably on his way to hibernation. Just getting in one last sunning in this warm weather."

The warmth was lost on Laura. A chill went over her when she thought about the man gunning for her and the snake that had come close to striking her. "I don't like snakes."

"I hear that." Paco checked her over, wiping at the dirt smudges on her cheek. "You have a scrape right there."

His finger stilled on her skin while their eyes locked

and held, the awareness between them a brief flare that warred with the sun and sent a new kind of chill down her spine.

Paco stepped back and turned to go to the man. Taking back his knife, he rubbed it through the sand then wiped it on a cactus stalk. Checking the man's pulse, he turned to Laura. "Yes, he's dead." Quickly going through the man's pockets, he pulled out a handgun and a wallet. "Howard Barrow. Do you know him?"

He heard her gasp then turned to see her rushing toward the man. "Howard? Did you say Howard?"

"Yes. Howard P. Barrow. According to his driver's license, he lives in Phoenix."

"He…he was my patient about a year ago."

"Really? No kidding?"

Her eyes burst into blue-tipped flames. "Why would I be kidding about this? Yes, he was a patient. He came to the clinic with a recommendation from… from Lawrence Henner. That was before Mr. Henner's son committed suicide and I got put on his blacklist."

"Okay, this is beginning to make me crazy," Paco said. At her disapproving look, he added, "Sorry. Crazy with *wondering*."

She stared down at the chubby, bleeding man. "Howard was a nice man. He worked for the government but he'd gone through a bad divorce and he had some emotional issues. We spent several sessions trying to get him through those issues. Last time I talked to him, he was dating again and happy."

"So a man who now blames you for his son's death once recommended you as a counselor to this man?"

"Yes." She pushed at her hair. "Poor Howard. This doesn't make any sense. He was a quiet, passive person who worked in records at the courthouse, not exactly someone who'd chase me through the desert."

"Something didn't get all the way cured in Howard, I'm thinking." And Paco also had another bad thought. "Better check his other pockets."

Laura wiped at her eyes while he dug around in Howard's jean pocket. "Just as I figured. He's carrying one of your outdated business cards." He held it up to the sun. "And it looks like the same indentations are on the back of it. Probably planned on leaving it with our dead bodies."

Her low groan brought Paco around. "What?"

"*What?*" She waved toward the dead man. "We're being stalked by the hour, Luke. You tell me. This man was a patient. What about the others? What about the man I shot?"

"Did you recognize him?"

"No, but it happened so fast I never actually got a good look and people change. They appear rough when I see them—lack of sleep and over or under eating, not to mention other indulgences. That man could have been someone I treated or spoke to in the clinic but he might have changed so much I didn't recognize him."

"When we get to Buddy's, I'll find out," he said. "Right now, we're too exposed. We need to get going."

"What about Howard?"

"What about him? He was going to kill us."

"He's dead now, though. We should do something."

"Look, we can't do anything. We don't have time and if we bury him it won't look so good for us. That whole hiding the body thing and all."

"So we just leave his body here for the vultures?"

"Do you have a better idea?" Cause he sure didn't.

She nodded. "We need to say a prayer over him and then, we need to call someone to come and get him."

Paco let a groan of his own. "Okay. You say a prayer and I'll text in a report to the sheriff."

And so he did. He explained the situation to his friend at the sheriff's department, giving him a location and a promise of a call later for more details. Then he stood silent while Laura said a prayer for the man who'd tried to take them both out.

When she was done, he tugged her along, marveling at her fortitude and her commitment to doing the right thing. "We're not waiting for the sheriff. Too dangerous. Let's go."

She followed him, beating a wide path around the coiled dead snake. "Was that a rattlesnake?"

"Yep. Looked like a western diamondback."

"You saved my life again."

"It's getting to be a habit."

Paco slowed down, thinking this woman had been through a lot for one day so maybe he should cut her some slack. But if they didn't hurry, the sun would go down on them in the desert. He did not want that to happen. He needed to get her to a safe spot so she could rest and digest all of this. And so he could call all the people waiting for him to give updates and reports. Everyone wanted answers. Well, so did he.

"Why would they bother leaving your card if they killed us?"

She pushed at her hair. "Maybe so whoever found us would also find the clues—if there are any clues on those cards."

"I'm guessing there's something on these cards."

He did a quick search of the area. "Of course, who-ever's behind this might have given the cards to his goons just in case they did get in trouble. That way, it looks like your patients had your business card—which would make sense and that would lead the authorities and CHAIM to think all of your patients were seriously deranged and chasing you all over the state to do you in."

"I'd have to quit work if that's the case. Maybe that's the point—to cause me to lose my license and my job."

He shot her a long hard stare. "We'll figure it out, Laura. While I don't exactly believe in therapy, I can see that you're probably good at your job. You seem to care about people. You went out of your way to find me."

She seemed to bask in that halfhearted compliment but she didn't push him. She was too numb and disturbed to try and break him down right now, Paco reasoned.

They walked in silence a few more miles, with the usual five-minute stops along the way.

"Not much farther now," he said after one of their breaks, hoping to help her along.

She didn't respond, but she got up and started walk-ing again. Paco hated the way she kept looking back at the spot where Howard Barrow had met his demise, even though they were a long way gone from that area.

After they'd walked a while longer, she said, "It doesn't bother you, does it?"

A lot of things bothered him. Especially pretty women in trouble in the middle of the desert. That and the growing body count bothered him a lot. The whole way his day had gone from self-imposed solitary confinement to wide open with visitors bearing guns bothered him. And the fact that his grandfather might be having surgery right now really bothered him. "What *doesn't* bother me?"

She missed the message in the question. "Killing people. It doesn't seem to bother you."

Paco grunted, but her words floored him. "You have no idea how it gets to me, trust me. And I'm not going to discuss that with you since we're not in your office and I'm not lying on the couch."

"But killing has become second nature to you. I saw the way you threw that knife. And killed that snake."

"Instincts, darlin'. I was trained to defend myself when I'm being attacked. I was trained to defend our country and to fight our enemies, both here and abroad. And I'd say we have several enemies on our back right now, right here in my backyard."

"No wonder you can't sleep."

Okay, the woman was tired, shocked and stressed. Paco knew all of those feelings. And in his gut, even though he knew she was being purposely harsh, he also knew she was right. He had become a machine. A killing machine. And her words cut to the quick with a pristine precision that caused him to lower his head and keep walking.

How was he supposed to reconcile that with the big guy in the sky? And how was he supposed to win this woman's respect when she'd witnessed him in action?

"Now I'm just like you," she said on a winded hiss. "I've killed another human being. And I'm beginning to think I'm responsible for all these people chasing us."

"Okay, enough!" He stopped as they made a turn on the path. "Just because you defended us this morning, doesn't make you like me. You will never be like me, understand? I can't help what happened today. Can't change what I've done in the past in the name of war. But I can save you if you let me—that's my job right now and that means I might have to hurt or kill other people in order to get you to safety. Will that be enough for you?"

She glared up at him, her face dirty and scraped, her eyes full of fury. And despair. "Enough for what?"

"Enough for you to forgive me?" he asked, his words going soft. "Enough for God to forgive me. You said God saved me for a reason and that you might be that reason. But not if you don't trust me and believe in me. And not if you can't forgive me." He held his hands on his hips and gave her a hard look. "I could use a little bit of forgiveness, okay?"

She looked up at him, the emotions boiling over in her misty eyes, a look of utter despair on her face. "It won't be you I'll need to forgive," she said on a raw whisper. "First, I have to forgive myself."

He shook his head. There was no reasoning with this woman. She had a shield of faith wrapped tightly around her true feelings. And now she was shouldering the blame for all of this and taking on his sins, too.

But Paco had a feeling once she let that shield down, let that guilt keep eating at her, she'd sink as low as he'd been at times. When that happened, someone needed to be there for her, the way she'd tried so hard to be there for her patients. And him.

Maybe God did have a plan after all.

Maybe Paco would have to be the one to pick up the pieces when Laura fell apart.

But that particular assignment scared him more than going into battle ever had.

* * *

He'd stopped walking just as the sun was setting off over a distant canyon rim. To Laura, it seemed as if they'd trekked over and over in the same circle for hours but Paco kept right on moving, stomping, marching. Did he actually know where they were going or was he as lost as she felt?

"There's my brother's house," he said.

Shocked and relieved, Laura glanced up to see the golden rays of the sunset striking against a small, flat adobe house that looked as if it had been perpetually added onto over the years. It leaned and sagged in places and grew and expanded in other places. And all around the yard, between yucca plants and tall cacti and iron-wood and desert willows, parts of cars and parts of motorcycles lay scattered like washed-out bones against the pinks and browns of the desert landscape.

"Interesting," she said on a dry-throated croak.

"Buddy's a mechanic of sorts but he's not known for being neat. Take that as a warning."

She didn't need to be warned. But when they got inside the house, she sure wished she could have stayed at that nice inn they'd left at the South Rim.

Paco must have seen her disgust before she could pull a blank face. "Keep in mind, he's in a wheelchair. He has a cleaning lady, but she only comes once a week. And he wasn't expecting company."

"It's okay. It's shelter." She sidestepped a stack of newspapers, pretty sure a scorpion ran across the floor when she did.

Paco turned on the kitchen light then stood as if wait-ing for the night creatures to scatter. "Kitchen looks reasonably safe. I'll find us something to eat."

Laura nodded, so tired she couldn't muster up conversation. In spite of the untidiness of the place, it wasn't dirty. There were clean dishes in the cabinets and the refrigerator was well stocked.

"Found some canned soup," Paco said. "Hope you don't mind another sandwich."

"I never ate my sandwich at lunch, so no, I don't mind."

He pushed past her. "Two bedrooms. I'll find sheets for the bed in that one." He pointed to a little room right off the den. "I'll keep watch here on the couch."

"You'll need to sleep, too."

"I don't sleep."

Then he whirled and turned on the bathroom light. "Towels are in the cabinet. I'll try to find you some clean clothes. I think Buddy's ex-wife left some here."

"He's divorced?"

"Yep. She couldn't deal."

"I'm sorry."

He grunted a response.

She noticed family pictures lining the wall. Men in uniform of various ages. "Your grandfather with your father?"

"Yeah. Wíago is my mother's father. My dad was part Hispanic. That was taken right before he left for Vietnam. He didn't make it home for Christmas. And he never knew about me." He shrugged. "He got killed before she could write and tell him."

"Where's your mother?"

"She died about five years ago."

"Did they live here in this house?"

"We've all lived here in this house at one time or another."

Laura's heart opened so wide she had to hold her rib cage tightly against her hands. What had this man suffered?

What had caused this house to become a sad replica of what it must have been when he'd grown up here with his brother? Had his mother raised them on her own after his father died in Vietnam?

So many questions she needed answering and so much hurt hidden behind smiling faces in faded photographs, in broken fragments of life covering the lonely, desolate yard.

And so much hurt hidden in the dark-as-night eyes of the man watching her now.

NINE

Paco watched Laura gather the clothes he'd found for her. Holding the sweater and jeans close, she went into the bathroom and shut the door.

What did she think of this house? Of him? Did she see the love that still lived here in spite of the shroud of shadows surrounding the rundown, lonely dwelling?

Did *he* still see the love they'd all once known here?

He immediately called Buddy. "How's he doing?"

"You know Wíago. He's tough as nails. Surgery went fine and barring no complications, he should be okay. At least that's what the doctors say."

His brother sounded tired, but Buddy had the same steely countenance of their grandfather. "Thanks for staying with him, Buddy."

"No problem, bro. Everyone's been nice here. I've got what I need and my friend who lives here says I can stay at his apartment if I want. And I'm even flirting with this one cute nurse—"

Paco stopped him right there. "Too much information. Just watch over him. And don't come back here until I give you the all-clear, okay?"

"Got it, but you know I can handle things on my end.

Don't worry about us, Paco. Do what you gotta do and take care, too."

They talked a few more minutes then Paco shut down his phone and went to the wide window of the little den to stare out into the dark night. A lone porch light was the only glow surrounding the midnight colors of the desert.

"It's been a while, Lord," he said, closing his eyes as he rested his forehead on the still warm glass. "I know I talk to You now and then when I get desperate, but tonight I hope You're truly listening to me. Wíago is in the hospital, Lord. He is innocent in this. If I brought this to our house, I ask forgiveness and guidance. If You brought Laura to me, I thank You and ask for a clear understanding. Protect my grandfather, protect my brother and protect Laura and me, Lord."

He opened his eyes, instincts forcing him to squint into the night. Was someone out there right now, just waiting? The desert, as silent and stoic as it seemed at times, was always alive and teeming with life. It could be a dangerous place, even when a person wasn't being tracked or stalked.

What human dangers lay out there?

He heard a crash in the bathroom and hit the floor running. "Laura, are you all right?"

At first, she didn't answer. He didn't hear the water running either. "Laura?"

His heart drummed like a warrior's cry against his ribcage. "Laura, I'm coming in—"

"No, don't. I'll be out in a minute. I'm okay."

But she wasn't okay. He could tell by the tremble in her voice she was probably having the meltdown she'd held at bay all day long. Paco respected her privacy while he paced across the expanse of the den.

When the door finally crept open, he hurried toward her. "Laura?"

She looked up at him, her eyes red-rimmed and swollen. "I'm sorry."

"Why? What are you sorry for?"

"For ever coming here in the first place."

Her sobs bubbled over and she put her hands to her face. "I didn't want to cry. I tried not to cry." She was shaking all over. "But I've never killed anybody. I've never even seen anybody killed before today."

Paco grabbed her up and took her to the old couch then found a patterned blanket to put around her. The clothes he'd found were a bit big on her, making her look even that much smaller.

"C'mon," he urged, settling her down on a pillow. "Just rest. The soup's ready and I'll make the sandwiches."

"I can't eat."

"You have to eat."

He started to get up, but she reached out to him. "Don't go yet. Sit here with me for a minute."

Paco sank back down on the far end of the couch. But Laura had other ideas. She scooted toward him then glanced up at him with those big blue eyes.

And he was lost.

With a resigned grunt, he gave in and tugged her close. "Shh. Just rest."

Laura leaned her head into the nook of his arm, forcing him to settle against her. It had been a long time since he'd comforted a woman. A very long time.

"I don't think—"

She shook her head against his chest. "It's all right,

Paco. I'm not…we're not…I don't expect anything. I just needed something to hold on to for a little while."

And she'd picked him.

Paco didn't know how to react. She only wanted comfort. And he didn't actually understand how to give anyone comfort. He was rusty in that department. But he knew all about respecting women, so he held her there and let her cry on his shoulder just to prove to her that she could trust him, that she was safe with him.

He had somehow become this strong, brave woman's reluctant protector.

God truly did work in mysterious ways.

Laura woke up, her breath heaving in her chest. She'd dreamed about a snake. Then she remembered everything that had happened, including the snake.

Sitting up on the couch, she looked around and saw Paco watching her from the tiny kitchen table. "Soup's still warm," he said, getting up to ladle her some into a big cup. "It's just tomato soup so you can sip it."

"Thanks," she said on a raspy voice. She'd sobbed every ounce of emotion out of herself and now she felt torn and raw, sore and empty. "How long did I sleep?"

"A couple of hours."

She took a sip of the warm soup. "Have you heard anything from your brother?"

He nodded. "Wíago got through the surgery. The doctor thinks he'll pull through unless we get any surprises such as blood clots, a stroke, or cardiac arrest. My grandfather is tough so I'm counting on that."

Laura could see the worry in his eyes. "And Buddy? Is he coming back here?"

"No. He's staying with a friend near the hospital. I

told him it might not be safe to return here by himself." He shrugged. "And he reminded me he was a weapons expert in the army."

Laura sat up and drank more soup. The spicy tomato taste washed over her throat and warmed her insides. "I should call my folks, let them know I'm okay."

"Already done."

"You called them?"

"No, Warwick did. He gave them only the necessary information—that we thought you had a stalker and you're with me until we can get you either back to Phoenix or to Eagle Rock."

"How are they?"

"Upset and concerned, but glad you're okay." He got up to come and sit on the split-log coffee table. "I have information that might explain a lot of this."

"I'm listening." She sat her soup cup down on the side table. "Tell me."

"We've found a pattern regarding the two people who've died today. They were both your patients at one time and they both have connections to Lawrence Henner."

"Even the one I shot?"

"Yes. He came to you about two years ago with post-traumatic stress syndrome. John Rutherford, retired marine. Ring a bell?"

Laura closed her eyes, nodding as she put a hand to her temple. "Yes. He was high maintenance, with major anger management issues. He abused his wife and even after we'd counseled him, he kept right on abusing her. He went to jail."

"And got out about two months ago."

"I can't believe I didn't recognize him."

He gave her a level look. "I'm pretty sure he disguised himself."

"What's going on?" she asked, pushing at her hair. "Is every patient I've ever failed coming after me now?"

"Looks that way on the surface," he replied. "Here's what we know for now—they both had emotional issues of some sort and they both came to your clinic for help. We're pretty sure Rutherford was the first shooter. When he failed the first time, he high-jacked the delivery truck. The driver was found unconscious on the road. He can't remember much about his attacker, but he described Rutherford. Rutherford's record fits the mode but his aim was a bit off today. And you probably didn't recognize him because his hair was longer and almost completely gray. He'd lost weight, too."

"I should have realized—"

"Laura, somebody out there doesn't want you to realize anything. They're playing mind games with you. I checked the two cards and rubbed a pencil over the indentions we thought we saw—links to Bible passages in Revelations."

"Revelations? But why?"

"Who knows? The person or people behind this aren't exactly rational. The first one is from chapter one, verse eighteen: 'I have the keys of Hades and Death.'"

"That's the Lord talking through John."

"Not in this case. Some madman is using the Lord's words to taunt us."

"What kind of keys?"

"We don't know. It might not mean anything."

"What about the second one?"

"From the second chapter, verse two: 'And you have

tested those who say they are apostles and are not, and have found them liars....'"

Laura's stomach roiled with each word. "Do you think this person is talking about me?"

Paco sat with his hands on his knees. "Again, we don't know. But we do know that these two men recently became employed by Lawrence Henner. You said he's a wealthy businessman? Well, we found out he owns his own security company—listed under some sort of corporation—a shell company. I think you mentioned something about that, too."

She let out a gasp. "No, I mentioned that Alex Whitmyer worked for a security company. What if it's Henner's company?"

"That could be bad. Very bad. Just one more connection though." He tapped into his phone. "I'll put Kissie on it." After explaining a possible connection between Henner and Whitmyer to Kissie, he hung up. "If they're working together, we can stop them."

"Could Alex be in this thing with Henner? That would mean they're both more unstable than I realized. Henner could be fueling Alex's obsession with me so he can come after me for my part in his son's death."

Paco looked grim. "According to data we've found underneath all the corporate logos, Henner does things in a much different way from CHAIM."

Laura could believe that. "He struck me as being demanding and unyielding, and honestly, I think that's why his son killed himself." She couldn't say anymore. Or maybe she should. "Paco, he verbally abused his son. And now he blames me for Adam's death. I never could prove that he was the one at fault because his son never told me the complete truth. But I believe that in my heart."

"So he's coming after you for justification?"

"Or to ease his own guilt?"

"Then why the card tricks?"

Laura shook her head, fatigue and alarm warring inside her mind. "He could be sending assassins, thinking we'd never trace it back to him. The first one didn't kill me, so he sent another one. Maybe the cards are his way of telling me what I've done wrong. Or his way of sending a message that there'll be more killings and attacks to come."

Paco got up, rolled his shoulders. "Except you didn't do anything wrong. He never demanded any type of settlement? Never came after you or the clinic with lawyers?"

"Lawrence Henner doesn't believe in lawyers. He always told me he liked to handle things his own way. And his son Kyle confirmed that over and over by refusing to open up to me. He was afraid of his own father."

"That's a big clue," Paco said. "He's obviously handling this in his own way. And controlling a possible small army of followers."

"And two men are dead because of it. Not to mention your grandfather almost dying, too."

"It's not your fault. You have to remember that."

"So what do we do now?"

"We keep putting the pieces together. Kissie's got the whole CHAIM team on this one. They've all gathered early at Eagle Rock for the so-called retreat, so they're brainstorming ways to get to the bottom of this."

"The whole team. I don't merit that, but it's good to know."

"You do merit that, Laura. You've helped countless people find better lives, grow stronger in their faith. This lone black sheep has obviously strayed from the flock, sweetheart." He whirled to stare down at her. "Or he was never part of the flock to begin with."

Then he sat down again and took both her hands in his. "But make no mistake. He brought this to my door and I won't stop until I have him behind bars."

"That could be very dangerous, Paco."

"Nothing for you to worry about."

"Right. Good one."

He touched a hand to her face, his smile sharp-edged. "We can't locate Henner. He's not in Phoenix and he's not in Austin. He must be out of the country, as you said."

"But someone's sending these men after us. Alex, maybe?"

"He might be Henner's right-hand man. It might take a while if he's hiding something, Kissie will find it."

"*He's* hiding while he sends these killers. His paranoia would certainly fit that mode."

"Killers who aren't very highly trained—bad for them but a blessing for us."

"Or the curse Henner wanted on us," she replied, a shudder gripping her with dread. But underneath that dread, a sense of dignity and integrity took hold of her. And a sense of justice. "They won't get away with this, Paco."

"No, sweetheart, they won't. I promise you that."

Laura took a deep breath then looked across at him.

"I'm done with falling apart. I'm done with crying. We have to stop this, you and me. I won't let you hide me behind the gates of Eagle Rock. I want to help find this man. I'm not scared anymore. And I refuse to be a victim."

TEN

The next morning, Paco stood at the window once again, coffee cup in hand as he thought about their next move. And the next move of the apparent madman after Laura.

She'd slept much of the night in the tiny bedroom just off the den while he'd kept watch on the couch, guns all around him, a trip wire set up on the front and back doors.

He'd dosed now and then, but since he was used to surviving on very little sleep, he'd never fallen completely to sleep. Too on edge. Too many images of death all around him. He'd sleep again one day. Maybe.

Right now, he had to map a way out of this desert and on to Texas. His gut told him the only safe place for Laura right now was Eagle Rock. And Warwick and the rest of the team agreed. His four team members— Devon Malone, Eli Trudeau, Brice Whelan and Shane Warwick had gone ahead of their families to Eagle Rock to go over the annual updates required by CHAIM. They'd also tested the overhaul on the security system, something that happened on an annual basis to protect those who came and went in the big security complex. Everything from iris and fingerprint scanners to updated digital equipment and big-brained computers had been tested and retested. But certain people knew how to overcome all of those things. Was Lawrence Henner one of those certain people?

"She should be safe here, Warrior," Eli had assured him on the phone earlier. "I'm bringing Gena and Scotty here in two days, so that should tell you something."

That did tell him everything. Eli Trudeau wouldn't put his new wife or his child in jeopardy. Nor would Devon, Brice or Shane, all so lovesick they'd protect those they held dear at all costs. Devon's wife, Lydia, was expecting their first child in a few weeks but she'd be at Eagle Rock, too. And Brice and his wife, Selena, would be together at Eagle Rock next week. Selena's father was a superior in CHAIM. Shane Warwick had married Katherine Atkins in England but he'd be remarrying Katherine, the daughter of CHAIM founding member Gerald Barton, again here in the States. They planned to repeat their vows sometime in the spring. But for the next week, they'd all be gathered there in the huge private complex, happy and secure while they celebrated Veteran's Day and Thanksgiving.

It sounded like a good place to leave Laura. Especially since she'd gone from broken and afraid to determined and mad. Not good in a woman even on the best of days.

"I need you to take her in then," he'd told Eli and Shane in a conference call. "I'll get her there but I'm not staying."

"Mandatory," Eli interjected.

That, coming from the original rogue agent.

Paco quickly retorted, "I didn't sign up. I don't have a family so I don't need a retreat or a self-imposed vacation. I need to work. That's what I need to do. I have to get to the bottom of what's going on with Laura Walton. Don't you think that overrides a retreat at Eagle Rock?"

"Hmm. Maybe," Warwick the Brit quipped. "The man does have a point, Eli."

"*Oui,* he does at that, my friend," the Cajun said in a low growl. "We'll protect the woman and let the Warrior do the hard work. Sounds like a solid plan to me."

So that was the plan for now. Paco would get Laura to the safe house and he'd get to the work at hand. Starting with tracking down Lawrence Henner. The man was as slippery as a desert snake. But like any snake in the grass, he'd strike again. And sooner than later, Paco figured.

If they had the right man, of course.

He heard a door opening and turned to find Laura dressed, but bleary eyed. Thinking about how she'd fit so nicely in his arms there on the couch, Paco did a mental shrug to let go of that notion. He didn't get involved. Ever.

Just find out who's after the woman, he reminded himself. All that touchy-feely stuff last night has to be left behind this morning. You offered her some comfort on the worst day of her life.

"Good morning," she said as she headed to the coffee pot. "Have you heard anything from your grandfather this morning?"

"Yes. He had a good night. The doctors believe he'll be okay. Buddy is going to hang around near the hospital to make sure."

She drank a sip of the rich coffee. "This is good."

"Grandfather's special blend. He orders it for the restaurant from a friend in Columbia."

"That explains why the café's coffee is so strong."

"But good for you," he said with a smile.

"Right now, I agree." She sipped it again, her hands clutching the heavy brown mug. "I'll need the jolt."

"You need to eat," he said, moving toward the tiny kitchen, the scent of the spicy shampoo she'd used to wash her hair surrounding him. "I made toast and bacon."

She watched him, her gaze weary and almost shy. Was she thinking about last night, too? Did she regret turning to him?

"Thanks." She picked up a crispy strip of bacon and nibbled at it. "What do we do now?"

Paco managed to look at her, trying to gauge whether she was travel-ready or not. "We're going to hike out of here and find the vehicle CHAIM is leaving for us at a gas station near a back road out of the state."

"Hike? But why?"

"Well, for starters, we don't have a car. Besides, our pursuers might be able to track us easier in a vehicle. And because I can track them better if they try following us through the desert."

"Won't that be dangerous?"

"Not any more dangerous than driving out of here. The desert protects its own. And I was born and raised here."

She shot him a look that indicated he was just that wild, too. "If you say so."

"I do." He had to be curt with her to regain control of oh-so-many emotions. "You need to follow my directions, no matter what."

"Even if I don't agree with your directions?"

"Even so. You're still alive, right?"

She shuddered, her fingers tightening on her coffee mug. "Yes, thank you."

Paco hated the hurt in her expression but he had to protect her, not make nice with her. Today would be hard on both of them. But he had to keep her enclosed in the landscape so they could get out of here alive.

"They found us yesterday," she said by way of an argument.

"Yes, but we were on a familiar trail. And the man they sent didn't succeed in killing either of us, in spite of that."

"Good point."

"Are you up to this then?"

"You mean walking around in the hot, dry, scary desert? I guess I don't have a choice."

"We can sit here and get caught or we leave," he retorted, grumpy with trying to focus on the work and not her pretty eyes. "My mission is to get you to Texas, sweetheart." He held up a hand. "I know you don't like that idea, but we're going there first."

"And then what?"

He took her mug and put it in the sink. "And then, I go to work to put a stop to this, one way or another."

Laura wondered about that one-way-or-another stuff.

She knew how CHAIM operated. The secretive security organization had agents scattered all over the world and for the most part, the agency went by its own code. Try to keep people alive, if possible. Don't break the law. Report to and hand over information, informants or suspects to the local, national or world authorities as needed. And always, always protect the subject, no matter what.

She'd never dreamed she'd be one of those subjects. She'd helped heal agents, victims, family members and innocent bystanders. Now she could wind up trying to heal herself instead of Luke Martinez. What a strange twist on her mission of mercy.

She didn't want him to be her protector.

But she sure felt safe knowing that he was.

Even if her protector was in one of his bad moods. Maybe he wasn't a morning person. Or maybe he was distancing himself after witnessing her humiliation as she fell apart right there in his arms last night.

The ugly truth looked so harsh in the glaring light of morning. And Luke Martinez was a harsh, tormented man. He'd only been kind to her so she could get through her own terrors from the day before. This was a new day and the man was on a new mission. She'd become his unwelcome burden. Now he had to deal with her and get on with things.

"I can help you with that," she said now as he moved with lightning fast efficiency around the house, gathering supplies for another trek through the heat and dust and prickly bushes and crawling critters of the unforgiving desert.

"Good. Look in that tall cabinet by the stove. That's the pantry. Look for disinfecting wipes, bandages and a box of energy bars. There should be a bottle of water purification tablets in there. Buddy keeps hiking supplies."

"Buddy? I thought he was in a wheelchair."

"He is. But he has a fancy motorized contraption.

Takes it out for day hikes." He shrugged. "He'd need supplies if something happened."

"Oh." Laura rummaged through the overstuffed pantry, finding most of what he'd asked for. "Do you want me to put these in one of the backpacks?"

"Set it all on the counter. I'll have to pack tight."

"I can carry my own."

"You'll have a smaller one." He must have seen her frown. "Look, you're not acclimated to this type of hike. We'll have to keep moving as much as possible."

She couldn't argue with that. "You're right. I've only gone on casual day hikes with friends. And usually on well-traveled paths." She fully expected him to take her off the beaten path. In oh-so-many ways.

Wanting to get to know him better, she asked, "Are you and your brother close?"

"Not every day."

She smiled at that. "I used to fight with my brother and sister all the time."

He grunted a reply of sorts.

"What do you do around here? I mean, since you got home?"

Another grunt, then a direct stare. "Well, up until yesterday, I didn't do much of anything. Just helped Grandfather around the café and stayed to myself."

Laura could almost feel the pointed emphasis of that statement. "I guess I messed up your sabbatical from CHAIM."

"I guess you did."

"How far do we have to go today?"

He stopped packing, his expression as blank as the rocks and dirt outside the door. "As far as we need to, sweetheart, to keep you alive."

Laura fell silent, wondering when this would end. Wondering why it was happening in the first place. Did Lawrence Henner have her on some sort of hit list? Thinking back to her counseling sessions with his son Kyle, Laura wished she could have done more for the boy. But then, Kyle was so afraid of his father he refused to open up to her no matter how much she pushed. Did she push too far?

Her guilt regarding Kyle Henner had tripled since coming here. And so had her feelings of stupidity regarding Alex Whitmyer. How could she have believed his pretty lies? She should have seen the truth sooner. So much for trying to heal herself. Had her actions brought this on Luke?

Lost in her dark thoughts, she didn't notice Luke standing there beside her until his hand touched hers. "Let me get you packed so we can go."

She looked up at him, all of her questions hushed for now. For just a minute, he looked so primal and hard-edged in his camo pants and green T-shirt, she almost stepped back.

"Here, put this on," he said, handing her a green canvas hat and a dark khaki long-sleeved shirt. "To hide you and to keep you from getting sunburned."

Laura took the garments, her breath hitching against her ribcage.

Luke Paco Martinez was in full combat mode.

And she pitied anyone who tried to get in his way.

ELEVEN

The man was loaded for bear.

Laura stumbled but regained her footing as they moved over the rocky terrain, her sturdy boots no match for the red sand and craggy rocks of the desert. Luke didn't seem to have the same problem. He moved like a shadow through the shrub brush and cacti, at times blending in so well with the land she found it hard to see him a foot ahead of her. And all of this with a heavy pack on his back.

"Need a break?" he asked, lifting his binoculars to take yet another panoramic scan of the land. They'd hiked up onto an outcropping of jagged rock that formed a wide mesa, giving them a clear view of the surrounding desert.

"I could use a drink of water," Laura replied, thinking silence with this man was just about as uncomfortable as a shouting match with her siblings. His silence shouted out at her with every twist and turn.

Taking a long swig of water from the canteen he shoved at her, Laura decided he had gone all non-communicative today because she'd gone all dramatic and hysterical last night. So much for finding a chink in his solid armor. Some men couldn't handle feminine theatrics.

Or maybe that was the problem. Maybe she had found the chink and he didn't like her seeing that side of him. If that was true, then at least she was on the right path. She'd just have to keep trying to get him to open up.

But how? It was like talking to a stone-faced mountain. This desert was easier to read than the man standing like an ancient chief in front of her.

"Are we still alone?" she asked then quickly amended. "I mean, besides the lizards, buzzards, chipmunks, snakes, spiders and scorpions?"

"No other humans," he said, dropping the binoculars back around his neck. Reaching for the canteen, he took a long drink.

That allowed Laura time to have a concentrated look at him. He lived up to his code name. He was a warrior, so fierce and so focused, she was afraid to sneeze.

"How far do we have to go?"

"About fifteen miles. It's not a long hike."

"Maybe not for you," she said, her tone mustering up an attitude. "Haven't we gone that far already?"

Paco turned to give her a once-over. "Are you faint? Do you feel light-headed?"

Only when I look at you, she wanted to retort.

"No, I'm fine. Just hot. You'd think with the temperatures in the sixties, it would be nice and pleasant."

"Not when you're moving and not with the sun shining on this dry land. So let me know if you feel a heat stroke coming on."

Did she detect a bit of condescension in that tone?

"I'm fine. Let's go," she shot back, determined to show him she could handle a mere fifteen more miles.

A few saguaros later, Laura decided to pass the time analysis style. "So you've lived here all your life?"

"Yep."

"Tell me about your dad?"

She saw him stiffen. "He died in Vietnam. My mom was pregnant with me."

"So you never even knew him."

"No. Just from pictures and memories. Only, she didn't like to talk about him much."

Laura let that soak in. "But you and Buddy, you seem to be close. I mean, do you two talk about things?"

He pivoted, his dark eyes hitting her like a sandstorm, all brittle and biting. "If you mean, do we share war stories, the answer is no. Soldiers don't like to talk about such things."

"Really," she said on a sarcastic note that she instantly regretted. "I know it's difficult, Paco. But since we don't have anything else to do—"

"I have something to do. I'm trying to get you to safety."

"Oh, so that means you can't be distracted, right?"

"That's right."

His dark frown ended that conversation.

They stomped on for a while. Laura scooted around another scorpion, groaning as the spindly creature lifted up from the dark shade of a prickly pear cactus and hurried across the desert floor.

"What?" Paco said, glancing over at her. He's insisted she try to stay beside him instead of behind him.

"A scorpion. He went the other way."

"Maybe he's afraid you'd analyze him, too."

Laura shot him a glaring look then saw the tilt

of his lips. "Are you actually making a joke at my expense?"

"I guess I am at that."

"Well, don't bust a gut laughing."

"I'm not laughing—on the outside."

This time, he actually smiled. It was such a pretty sight, Laura wanted to grab him and hug him tight. Or at least grab on to something as that light-headedness he's mentioned seemed to hit her. But she refrained from that since everything out here in the desert was prickly. Including the man.

"I'm glad I can at least make you smile," she said.

"I don't have anything better to do."

"Except protect me as you've reminded me over and over. I mean, that is why you're being so surly, right? I interrupted your quiet self-imposed isolation and you're not very happy about that. And I guess you're not happy about getting shot at and about your truck getting messed up and especially about your grandfather being hurt."

"Nope. Not happy about any of that." He stopped, put his hands on his hips and leveled her with one of his fierce looks. "But I am happy that scorpion went the other way because I don't have time to nurse you if you get bitten."

"I'm so touched by your consideration."

"Don't mention it."

"How do you know which way to go?" she asked, fascinated by how he would take a turn without even missing a step.

"I do have a compass," he pointed out, showing her one of many cords around his neck. "And I watch the barrel cactus. If you notice, they tend to tilt toward the south."

She hadn't noticed. Now Laura had something to concentrate on, at least. So she started watching for any barrel cacti, noting that some of them grew to four feet tall. "So we're going south?"

"Bingo."

She let out a sigh, wishing the man liked to chatter as much as she did. Then something up in the sky caught her attention. "Oh, look."

Paco glanced up to where she pointed. A lone hawk spiraled through the clouds like a dancing warrior.

"He's so beautiful," Laura said, shading her eyes even though her hat provided a little shade.

Paco didn't say anything. He nodded and moved on.

And then the hawk swooped down and went in for the kill. When he lifted up, he had a fat desert rat in his talons.

"Beautiful and deadly," Laura said, her enthusiasm and interest taking a dark turn. "I need to remember it's survival of the fittest out here."

Paco didn't respond. But she did see him glance over at her, a look of apology on his face.

"We're here," Paco told Laura a couple of hours later. Thankfully, she'd become quiet the last few miles of this trek. She had to be exhausted, but she'd been a trooper. He admired her determination.

"I see civilization," she said, happiness shining in her eyes. "I can't wait to have a nice long shower."

"That might be a while. This is just the first part of our journey."

He ignored her groan and instead concentrated on scoping the tiny village where Shane told him a used

We'd like to send you two free books to introduce you to the Love Inspired® Suspense series. These books are worth over $10, but they are yours to keep absolutely FREE! We'll even send you 2 wonderful surprise gifts. You can't lose!

REMEMBER: Your Free Merchandise, consisting of **2 Free Books** and **2 Free Gifts**, is worth over $20.00! No purchase is necessary, so please send for your Free Merchandise today.

Plus TWO FREE GIFTS!

We'll also send you two wonderful FREE GIFTS (worth about $10), in addition to your 2 Free Love Inspired Suspense books!

YOUR FREE MERCHANDISE INCLUDES…

2 FREE Love Inspired® Suspense Books

AND 2 FREE Mystery Gifts

FREE MERCHANDISE VOUCHER

2 FREE
BOOKS
and
2 FREE
GIFTS

Please send my Free Merchandise, consisting of
2 Free Books and **2 Free Mystery Gifts.**
I understand that I am under no obligation to buy
anything, as explained on the back of this card.

*About how many NEW paperback fiction books
have you purchased in the past 3 months?*

❏ 0-2
EZT4

❏ 3-6
EZUG

❏ 7 or more
EZUS

❏ I prefer the regular-print edition ❏ I prefer the larger-print edition
123/323 IDL   110/310 IDL

FIRST NAME	LAST NAME

ADDRESS

APT.#	CITY

STATE/PROV.   ZIP/POSTAL CODE

NO PURCHASE NECESSARY!

◀ DETACH AND MAIL CARD TODAY! ▶

(LISUS-FM-10R)

® and ™ are trademarks owned and used by the trademark owner and/or its licensee. © 2009 Steeple Hill Books. Printed in the U.S.A.

pickup from a local dealer would be waiting. Shane had arranged that over the Internet and phone, so Paco trusted their mode of transportation would indeed be here.

He stopped Laura before they emerged onto the lonely road cutting a patchy gray ribbon through the craggy hills.

"Okay, here's the deal. See that gas station over there."

She nodded. "The one with the red stripes."

"The only one in town, sweetheart."

"Got it. Gas station."

"See the blue truck parked by the road?"

"Yes. Is that our truck?"

"Should be. Let me see if I can get a line out to Eagle Rock." He pulled out his phone and hit an app. "Signal looks good."

While he waited for Shane to answer, he said, "Drink," and shoved the canteen at her. Then he motioned toward her small backpack. "Eat a power bar."

Laura rolled her eyes, but did as he asked.

The Knight answered on the first ring. "Warwick."

"We've made it. Blue truck?"

"That's the one. The keys are under the seat."

"How high-tech of you."

"It's the middle of nowhere, old boy. And it was the best deal I could make over the net."

"Looks like a keeper."

"Did anyone follow you?"

"Not that I can tell. Everything's cool right now."

"Good. But, Warrior, I need to tell you something. You might want to keep this information from Laura. I'll let you decide."

"Shoot."

"We think we've located Laura's missing laptop. Kissie zoomed in on the tracking device."

"You can do that?"

"Kissie can, yes. She found a weak signal. And that's the odd part."

"Keep talking."

"The signal is nowhere near the desert, Paco. The laptop seems to be in Texas now."

Paco glanced over at Laura. She was stubbornly chewing on her power bar. "I understand."

"Didn't you say Henner owns an estate in Texas?"

"Affirmative."

"Interesting, don't you think?"

"Extremely. I'll bear that in mind."

"Right. And we'll keep trying to get to the bottom of this, maybe scout out his property here. The signal comes and goes which means he's still on the move. If he tries to break into any files, Kissie might be able to check the IP addresses to get the local network topology. She can encrypt the data, possibly."

"That Kissie is amazing."

"That she is. You take care. 'The eyes of the Lord are in every place, keeping watch on the evil and the good.'"

"Proverbs," Paco said, understanding his friend wanted him to use his own eyes for Laura's safety. "I hear you, Knight." Then he asked, low, so Laura wouldn't pick up on it, "And what about Alex Whitmyer?"

"Interesting about that one," Warwick replied. "We got a hit on his fingerprints because he works in security, and possibly because he was booked a few years ago for harassment charges. They were dropped, apparently.

He does indeed work for Lawrence Henner. He's one of Henner's top men. In fact, he's the one in charge while Henner is out of the country. Did subject happen to mention that?"

"I don't think subject knows that."

He heard Warwick let out a long sigh. "This is a very odd case, Paco. Too many variables and way too much coincidence."

"There are no coincidences," Paco retorted.

He put the phone away and wondered if he should tell Laura about this latest development. Why was her laptop coming onto the radar in Texas? And exactly when did the man who'd stalked her start working for Lawrence Henner?

What was so important about her files that someone would take her laptop across the Southwest and into another state?

And was the threat to her now over?

So many questions and each one holding some sort of danger for Laura.

"Is everything all right?" Laura asked, her eyes holding his.

"Everything is just fine," Paco retorted. He'd get her in the truck and on the road and then maybe he'd tell her about the missing laptop's whereabouts.

And about her ex-boyfriend's brush with the law and his interesting employment record.

TWELVE

The truck was loud and without air or heat.

Unless Laura counted the heat in Paco's gaze each time he glanced in the rearview mirror or looked over at her.

The weather was mild so she wasn't too miserable. But she was pretty sure the man driving was full of misery. He didn't want to be here, but his sense of duty obviously trumped any personal feelings he might have. Including how he might feel about her, she decided.

"Are we being followed?" she asked after an hour of his famous silence.

"No."

"Are you mad at me?"

"No."

"So you're just not a big talker, right?"

"Right."

This didn't set well with Laura. She needed him to talk to her, and not just so she could find out information about him. She needed to hear his voice to keep calm, to keep from screaming in sheer terror, to keep the memory of that man she'd killed out of her mind. If she talked, she could forget how the man's eyes opened in a vacant stare or how the touch of his death still stained her with guilt and grief.

"I need you to talk to me," she said. Putting a hand to her mouth, she added, "I didn't mean to say that out loud."

"What do you want to talk about?" he asked through what sounded remarkably like a snarl.

"I don't know. What kind of movies do you like?"

"Don't go to the movies very much."

"If you did go, what kind of movie would you want to see?"

He sat so silent, she wondered if he'd even heard her. Then he finally said, "Film noir."

Laura did not see that coming. "So you like classic movies better than modern-day ones?"

"I guess I do. Used to watch them with Wíago a lot. He liked movies with Humphrey Bogart and Cary Grant and all the John Wayne Westerns, but I think he loved Lauren Bacall and Grace Kelly—pretty women in pretty clothes. He also read a lot of detective novels and passed them on to me. We didn't have a lot of money to buy new books."

Laura catalogued the remark about pretty women. She didn't fit into that sophisticated category but she wondered if that was the type Paco liked, too. He didn't seem to be all that urbane but then that was why she was asking questions. "What about music?"

He shifted the gears as he made a turn. "I guess I can tolerate country music—the good old-fashioned country music. And I like classical music, too."

"Classical? I wouldn't have pegged you for that."

Another surprise. Next he'd tell her he had a tuxedo tailor made and as fine as any Shane Warwick would wear.

He gave her a slanted look. "What? I don't fit the bill?"

"Not exactly."

"Wíago traded some of his sculptures once for a whole batch of Bach, Beethoven and Mozart records. We used to crank it up and sit out on the porch and look at the stars. That music would drift out over the desert and soothe the lizards and snakes, even the coyotes, I think."

"Did it soothe you?"

"It did. It used to."

She noted that. "I love classical music, too. I use it a lot at the clinic. But I also love rock and roll."

"Wouldn't have pegged your for that," he retorted, mimicking her earlier words. "You're full of surprises."

"So are you."

"Me?" He slanted a look toward her. "What you see is what you get."

Was that a warning to her? Laura figured he wasn't interested in her in any way, so she let that one slide.

"Can you tell me what Shane Warwick said to you on the phone?"

He shifted in his seat. What did he know? What was he not telling her? Laura tried to reassure him. "I can handle it, Paco."

Another hard glance told her he did have information he wasn't sharing with her. "Are you sure?"

"Of course. This is my life, after all. And we have a lot of hours left to get to Austin, by my calculations."

Taking another scan in the mirrors, he let out a sigh. "Your laptop has surfaced in Texas."

"Texas? How…when?"

"Kissie Pierre has ways of tracking just about anything issued by CHAIM. And that includes stolen laptops, cell phones, anything electronic. She did some finagling and got a hit. We think Henner might be back in the States and on his way to his home in Austin. Or someone working for him has it. It's all speculation right now, but it's the only lead we have."

"He probably had someone steal the laptop while he distracted us with all those attempts on our lives."

"Good point. Whoever took it messed up your room, maybe to make it look like a random robbery or to scare you."

"It worked. I don't have anything to offer these people."

"They took your laptop for a reason, though. If we can track the laptop, we might find our culprits. Or one of the culprits."

"Do you think they'll keep coming after me?"

"They could. If they only wanted information, well, they have that. If they come after us again, well, that means they want to make sure you don't talk."

"I don't have anything to talk about," she said, dread and frustration warring in her mind. "I can't imagine what they think I know."

"You know everything about your patients."

That stunned Laura. "You think they're going after my patients, too?"

"All I know for sure is this—two of your patients have tracked you and tried to kill you. They both worked for Henner and they're both dead now. And in spite of the fact that they were amateurs, it was either them or us, sweetheart. And the other thing I know for sure—your stolen laptop has all of your patient information on it." He stopped, his hesitation telling.

"What else did Warwick tell you?" she asked.

"You don't need to know everything, okay?"

"Yes, I do. I need you to be honest with me so I can deal with this. I'm not good with surprises."

He glanced in the mirrors, scanning each one in his own dear time. Finally, he looked at her. "Your ex-boyfriend Whitmyer works for Henner. Did you know that?"

Laura's breath caught while her heart raced ahead. "No. I wondered about that, remember? He was always vague about it because it was a security company. I even suspected he might work for CHAIM."

"He's never been with CHAIM, I can tell you that. Warwick thinks he must have signed on with Henner recently."

"Like—after we broke up?"

"Could be. Or maybe before he started dating you. We'll keep researching that angle."

"This goes from bad to worse."

"That's usually how criminals work."

Laura stared out as the landscape changed to more stark rocky mesas. They were nearing Albuquerque, New Mexico, and making record time since he was driving at full speed. He had somehow managed to avoid any state troopers.

"They might be after a specific person, but then that doesn't explain why they keep coming after us. If Henner and Alex are working together, this could go way beyond me, Paco."

"If they want patient information, they'd also want to kill you so you can't stop them from getting it. Or so you can't stop them from whatever it is they're trying to do."

Laura leaned her head against the cracked leather of the old truck seat. "I wish I could understand this."

"You and me both. But for now, we keep driving and we keep playing with any scenario you can think of. Any memories that trigger something, you let me know."

She wanted to say she'd do that for him if he'd do the same for her. The distraction of getting to the bottom of his torment would sure help her in trying not to think of her own. "I will," she said, wondering if she could come up with anything concrete.

Her eyes still closed, she thought back to the two men who'd been killed. What else about those two that could be a common thread? They were both in their early thirties, both had failed at other jobs and they'd both failed at relationships. What had become of them in between the time she'd treated them till yesterday when they'd died?

"Did Kissie happen to find anything on what our two shooters were doing recently?" she said, looking over at Paco. "Any employment issues or status changes, things such as that?"

"I can find out," he said, grabbing his phone out of the cup holder on the dash.

"Hey, Kissie. Yeah, we're okay for now. Question for you." He repeated what Laura had just asked. "I'll wait.

"She's checking," he reported to Laura. Then "Really? That's interesting, isn't it? Thanks. I'll tell Laura that."

"What?" Laura asked, hoping Kissie could help her.

"This is starting to make more sense, at least," he replied, his eyes on the road. "Both of these men *were* hired by a Central Security Network a few weeks after Kyle Henner died. But Alex Whitmyer has worked there for several years. He worked his way up to a top-dog and he's been in charge since Henner left the country. He's very knowledgeable regarding electronics and high-tech security systems."

Laura felt sick to her stomach. Her nerves roiled as the truck kept moving up the back road. "If Henner is trying to get even with me, Alex would be the perfect man to do it."

"Yes. So we can surmise that Lawrence Henner has hired former patients of yours, apparently to come after you and leave you calling cards with cryptic verses on them. And that he is also in cahoots with your former boyfriend, too."

Laura put her head in her hands. "He must really hate me. He does blame me for his son's suicide—that much I knew. I just didn't know he'd want revenge enough to kill me."

"Or take your private files. We still have to figure out why he's doing that."

"He might think he can find other patient cases where I failed."

"Are there others?"

"Not many. I can only do so much, but unless the patient is willing to follow our suggestions and recommendations regarding treatment and medication, I can't completely cure them."

"So do you think there might be others?"

Laura thought back over the few years she'd been at

the clinic. "We have a strong success rate, but we aren't one hundred percent as far as curing patients. I don't recall any other cases, though."

"Anything else about these two that might connect them even more?"

"If I had my files, I could check," she replied. "It's hard to say from memory alone."

"Think, Laura. There must be something we can use to keep putting the pieces together."

Laura sat silent for a few minutes. "I'm sorry. My mind has gone numb from all of this." Pushing at her hair, she let out a breath. "I'm tired, Paco. So tired."

"Sleep," he ordered. "Don't think about it anymore for now. Rest."

His orders didn't help matters but since she didn't know what else to do, Laura closed her eyes again and put her head back against the seat. The warmth from the winter afternoon was waning as sunset began to take over.

Paco tossed a jacket toward her. "Cover up."

He had such a way with words, she thought as she grabbed the camo jacket to wrap it against her arms and shoulders. When she immediately recognized his scent of sweat mixed with the spicy shampoo they'd both used back at his brother's house, Laura inhaled and tried to relax.

She didn't know when it had happened, but she felt safe with Paco Martinez. In spite of his gruffness and his unwillingness to talk about his own feelings and emotions, she knew he was a good man.

And that's all she needed to know. He'd protect her because he was a trained soldier. A reluctant hero. A man searching for his own heart.

Laura decided to pray for Paco while she tried to relax. And so she began, asking God to guide him and help him, to heal him and nurture him. Laura wanted Paco back in the fold. He might seem like a black sheep, but he was really just hurting and disillusioned by all the death and destruction he'd had to witness in the war.

If I can't help him, Lord, I know You can. Please guide Paco as he tries to protect me. Help him to find out who these terrible people are and what they want from us.

Laura kept going, her prayers changing as she thought about every detail of Luke Paco Martinez. She thought back over his life, over his army career and his time with CHAIM. He'd wanted to serve both his country in the military and CHAIM in the private security sector. And working for CHAIM meant Paco wanted to serve the Lord, too.

She'd learned a lot about him before coming to find him. She'd even downloaded some very high-security files on him, with CHAIM's permission since his case was active and highly sensitive. At least, she had somewhat of a handle on him even if he didn't want to talk to her.

That brought Laura even more comfort.

She was drifting off to sleep, her prayers on a perpetual spin inside her head, when she suddenly realized something very important about her two former patients.

"Paco," she said, lifting up so fast the big jacket fell to her waist. "I remembered something. Something so obvious I don't know why I didn't think of it before."

THIRTEEN

He pulled the truck off the road at a deserted farm-house then after doing a quick surveillance of the area, shut down the engine. If she'd figured out something significant he wanted to be sitting still when he heard it. "Go ahead. Tell me what you remembered?"

Laura inhaled then shook her head. "It might not mean anything but…Howard Barrow and John Ruther-ford had both applied to become CHAIM operatives when they were younger. And they both got turned down. I'm surprised Kissie didn't find that in her back-ground check."

Paco rubbed a hand over the beard stubble on his chin. "Applied? Most of us were invited to join or were nominated by an older member. Rarely does a person ask to join CHAIM because so few people know about the organization. Are you sure about this?"

She bobbed her head. "It's in their files. I can't believe I didn't make the connection sooner."

If anyone could understand repressed memories, it was Paco. He was running from his own. "That's okay. Stress can do that to a person and you certainly had no way of knowing this would come up again. But you're remembering things now, so keep talking."

She closed her eyes for a minute then looked at him. "We might be able to pull more information from my office hard copy if I can get to someone and explain why I need the information. Those files are confidential but this is an emergency situation." Then she put a hand to her mouth. "Unless of course, whoever took my laptop has erased that information."

"Good point, and possibly why Kissie didn't spot it." He held a hand on her arm. "Tell me more about these two. Why weren't they accepted?"

"Howard Barrow had a drug problem in his teens so he didn't past muster for what he called the 'elite, holier-than-thou group.' He was kind of bitter about it, but he only mentioned it once and in passing. And that's strange since he had no way of knowing I work with CHAIM employees. They're usually referred by church counselors."

"Is that how *he* came to you—from a church referral?"

"No. He was a walk-in."

"And what about John Rutherford?"

"He was a member of CHAIM for a year, right after he graduated from college. But he told me he didn't like the work." She shrugged. "That's all I can remember about him."

Paco thought back on the two men who'd come gunning for them. "Neither of them were pros, that's for sure. We're talking about late thirties, paunchy and, well, downright foolish if you ask me. If Henner sent them, he sure was asking for failure. But why would he want their CHAIM records erased?"

Laura tugged at the jacket in her lap. "And why in the

world would either of them do his bidding in the first place?"

Paco had to remind himself of how innocent this woman was. Innocent and naïve and too good to be caught up in this kind of mess. "Laura, some people will do just about anything for the right amount of money."

"Henner has lots of that."

"Yes, the man has money, power, several locations to hide out, and he runs a security company—that on the surface is somewhat like CHAIM."

"But *not* on the surface?"

"Not on the surface, something isn't right. I don't think our man Henner is using his powers for good."

"He's evil. I can believe that from talking to his son, and from seeing the way he blamed me for Kyle's death. If the man only knew. I do blame myself, but I also think Lawrence Henner pushed his son to the breaking point. And from what Kyle told me, he pushed his employees in much the same way. Kind of a vigilante tactic."

Paco reached over to push a strand of hair off her cheek. "Yes, he's got some kind of agenda—maybe a vendetta against you. He's after you for a reason, Laura. Maybe because of his son's death or maybe for another reason all together. You can't blame yourself for some whacked-out man's idea of justice."

"I'll always blame myself," she replied, looking away.

Paco understood a lot about her now. Had she come here to help him, hoping he wouldn't end up like Kyle Henner? "Look," he said, "if Henner is behind this, we'll get him. And this information is just another link.

I have to call Kissie and the others. They can research away while we try to get you there."

"And what about you?" she asked. "You keep telling me you're taking me to Eagle Rock, but you don't say anything about staying there yourself."

"I'm not planning on staying," he said while he waited for Kissie to answer. "I intend to find Lawrence Henner and ask him a few questions."

He heard Laura gasp, saw the denial in her eyes. Holding up a finger to quiet her, he said, "Kissie, how's everything?"

"The gang's all here. All except you, of course."

"I'm on the way to drop off the package."

He looked over at the package and saw that Laura was perplexed and a bit perturbed at him. It would have to do.

"Kissie, I have some new information." He reported what Laura had told him. "You might do another search to connect any of Laura's patients to both CHAIM and Henner's security company. See how many hits you get. We think Henner somehow erased that bit of information from Laura's files—possibly her laptop and any hard copy or backup files, too."

"I'm on it," Kissie said. "This is getting downright weird, Warrior."

"Yep. Where is the team today?"

"Where else? In the war room, trying to figure this thing out. You've handed us a fascinating case and it's rare these days that we're all in one place to solve it. Feels like the good old days when we all worked together."

"I can use the help, that's for sure."

"We'll be here. The family members are arriving

today. My son Andre will be here. He's so ready to start training to become an operative."

"Andre's that old?"

"Yes, sir, almost twenty-three. You know, you could stay here with Laura. I'm sure she'd feel better if you did. We'll solve this together, Paco. It's safe here."

Paco heard the undercurrent in her words. *Are you sure you're ready for this? Should you go out there on your own? Will you crack under the pressure?*

He didn't intend to crack and he prayed he wouldn't. He had to keep it together for Laura's sake.

"Nice try, Kissie. But I need to find out what Henner is up to. My first stop after Eagle Rock will be his estate in Texas. Any more on the laptop?"

"The signal comes and goes. But it's still in Texas."

"Okay. We've got to get a bite to eat and keep moving. I should have her there by midnight."

"We'll keep a light on for you."

Paco put his phone away then looked at Laura. "I know what you're thinking but I can't hide out at Eagle Rock. These people came after us, Laura. And my grandfather could have been killed. They put this at my doorstep so it's up to me to get to the bottom of things."

She sat up to glare at him. "And I'm the reason for that. I brought this to your door, Paco. I can't have your death on my conscience, too. Let one of the others go after him. Or take them all with you to find him."

"Not a bad idea," Paco said. "Just might work."

"Are you serious?"

He saw the hope in her eyes. And something else he didn't want to see. But he had to ask anyway. "Worried about me, sweetheart?"

She got all fidgety, her fingers working the frayed flap of his old camo jacket. She wouldn't look at him. "I told you, I don't want anyone else to die."

Of course she didn't. She was a good girl caught up in a bad situation. Nothing to do with pining for him. "No one else is going to die if I can help it. I'm not going to die and neither are you. That's the plan."

"But you will consider taking help—some backup? I mean you're part of a five-man team. It doesn't make sense to let four of them stand around doing nothing while you go in alone with guns blazing."

He put his hands on the steering wheels. "It *has* been a long time since we all went out as a team. Not since South America when we tried to bring that girl out of the jungle."

"And Eli's grandfather was behind her death and everything that happened to Eli. That was horrible. You were all betrayed. I don't want this to turn out that way."

"Neither do I," he said. "And if I know my team, they won't let me go alone. Unless I give 'em the slip, of course."

"No." She grabbed his arm, her gaze flaring hot. "Promise me you won't go without one of them at least."

Because he didn't want to think about the gentle tug of her touch or the tug inside his heart, Paco shook her away and cranked the truck. "You don't think I can do it alone, do you, Counselor?"

Shock colored her face. "I didn't mean it that way, but now that you mention it—are you ready for this?"

He hit the steering wheel. "Why can't anyone believe I'm okay?"

"Okay is one thing, Paco. But being sound in both body and mind is another. That's why I came to talk to you in the first place."

He shut his eyes, saying his own prayer of patience. "I don't need to spill my guts to anyone else. I went over everything with debriefing and army therapists. And I had a nice long stay in Ireland at Whelan Castle. I'm a soldier. This kind of thing comes with the territory."

"This kind of thing can push you over the edge, too. It's called post-traumatic stress and survivor's guilt and you have—had—a classic case of it."

Anger colored his next words but it felt good to be angry. "Yes, maybe I did but I'm good to go now. I've been to the edge, sweetheart. I won't go back there."

"Then don't take a chance on having to face that kind of pain again. Ask for help, Paco. There's no shame in that. That's why CHAIM has teams to begin with."

He couldn't argue with that. And he didn't want to go rogue and mess up the delicate balance of the CHAIM team he'd been a part of for years. He could be a hothead or he could keep a cool head. The difference could mean saving lives.

"I'll think about it," he said. Then he surprised himself. "I'll make you a promise. Once I get you safely inside the gates of Eagle Rock, we'll find a quiet spot and you can ask me anything you want. How's that?"

She didn't look as pleased as he'd hoped. "I don't need that kind of promise from you. I need you to be ready to deal with what happened to you in Afghanistan." Her shoulders lifted in a shrug. "Maybe now is not the time. You're already under a lot of pressure."

"What do you really want from me, Laura?"

Her eyes brightened with unspoken words. "I want you to heal. That's all. I want you to heal."

"Then give me time and let me do what I have to do. The only way I can function right now is by getting you to a safe place and figuring out what Henner is up to. That's what gives me strength. That's my job."

"Okay." She bobbed her head. "Okay. You're right. I came to see you for one reason and now, we have other things to consider. I haven't been fair in trying to make you open up to me in the midst of all of this."

If she only knew. He'd like nothing more than to turn this truck around and find some pretty spot so he could just talk to her, get to know her. But he couldn't do that tonight.

"Are you hungry, thirsty? Do you need a break?"

"I'm okay for now," she replied, quieting back into her corner as if she didn't want to provoke him. "I just want this to be over."

"You and me both," he replied.

Because if this didn't end soon, he would be in too deep to turn back. He might actually start caring about this woman. And that could be his downfall.

Midnight inked its way through the ribbon of winding back road. Laura woke up with a start to stare out the window, her disoriented mind searching for a reason why she might be sleeping in a moving truck. Then she turned and saw the hawkish features of the man driving her across the Texas Hill Country.

"Where are we?" she asked, her voice raspy and low.

He shot a glance toward her then turned back face

forward to stare at the road. "Almost to Austin. We should be at Eagle Rock in about an hour."

"We'll wake everyone up."

"Nah, they never sleep."

"Good point, since I've never actually seen you sleep."

For just a flashing second, Laura imagined what it would be like to have this man in her life in a normal way. A way where she fixed him breakfast and sent him off to a safe day job. A way where he came home to dinner and kissed her on the cheek.

She turned toward him and thought she saw an awareness rushing like a fast rain inside his mysterious eyes. Did he feel it, too? Did he feel the tug, the pull, of wondering what it would be like to have one normal day together?

Laura reminded herself that this man was a loner who lived a hard, dangerous life. He was broken and bitter and she couldn't hope to fix all of him. The counselor part of her could try to help heal his wounds, but her woman's heart urged her to fix the rest of him, to try and get inside his heart and not just his head.

But that was dangerous territory.

He gave her another glance. "Look, Laura—"

And then a piercing sound shot through the old truck and it started spinning out of control, air hissing out of a tire.

Paco grunted in surprise then pushed her down with one hand while he maneuvered the truck into the spin with the other hand. "Stay down and hold on!"

Laura's heart fell to her feet, the heavy pace of her pulse booming in her ears while her world spun like a top, memories and feelings flowing over her as the truck whirled and careened. In her mind, she was still waiting for him to finish his sentence. But he didn't.

She heard more shots, felt Paco's hand on her arm. He held the truck steady, cycling around and around, ducking his head now and then, then lifting up to glare into the mirrors. Rising up, Laura tried to see behind them.

"Don't move, Laura. Stay down!"

How could she possibly move now? Laura became frozen in a numb kind of panic. But inside that panic, her heart beat with a fierce need to stay alive. She wouldn't let this happen. She wouldn't let Paco give his life for her here on this dark road out in the middle of nowhere. And so she fought to hold on, fought through silent, screaming prayers, the touch of his hand guiding her.

It was only seconds, but in Laura's mind, this dizzying trip into the dark night went on and on. She could hear Paco's gruff complaints, see the control in his stoic face, and feel his fingers gripping her, holding her as the windshield shattered. Then she felt a piercing pain as the truck jolted up into the air, causing her to bounce up and right into the windshield, even while Paco managed to hold on to her arm.

Finally the groaning truck came to a shuddering stop, the sound of tires grinding into dirt and rock and shrubs sliding over Laura's ragged nerve endings with a hissing protest.

The shots had stopped. The truck rattled to a loud stillness. Her heart pumped and pushed inside her body, her breath came fast and furious and mingled with Paco's rapid breathing next to her. While the pain tried to pull her deeper and deeper into the darkness.

And still, his hand had never left her arm.

Through it all, Paco had held on to her.

FOURTEEN

Paco tugged at her. "Laura? Laura, are you all right?"

She nodded then lifted the jacket. "Paco?"

He saw the blood, a bright red stain moving over her sweater. Then he saw the hole in the jacket. He looked up, his gaze slamming into hers. Her face was pale in the moonlight, her eyes whitewashed with fear. And pain.

She'd been hit.

Still holding her, he reached into the bucket seat behind his seat and grabbed his gun, placing it on the dash. Then he felt around for the first aid kit.

"Hang on. Laura, do you hear me? Hang on." He touched two fingers to her neck, prayers screaming in silence inside his head. He had to do something. He had lots of supplies, but nothing to stop this kind of bleeding. Throwing the kit back behind the seat, he pulled on her sweater and saw the tiny bullet hole piercing her left upper shoulder.

"I'm okay," she said, grabbing at her sweater. "It's just a little cut or something—probably from the glass. Let's go. Just go."

"I can't go until I know how bad you are." He pulled a

T-shirt out of his duffel. "Can you hold this tight against your wound?"

She gave him a feeble nod. "Uh-huh."

"Where does it hurt?"

"Everywhere. Mostly my left arm."

Paco did a quick scan of her body, touching on her head, neck and shoulders and working his fingers on her legs. "No other injuries that I can find."

"Nope. Just a bump on my head and a hole in my arm." She swallowed, her eyes closing in a squint of pain.

"I'm going to lift you," he said, gently reaching behind her. "So I can see if the bullet went through."

She nodded, gritted her teeth.

Paco reached behind her, his arms around her shoulders. "Hold on."

She moaned as he lifted her forward and let her fall against his chest. "There's no tear in the seat and you're not bleeding on your back." He might have to dig the bullet out. "Okay, I'm gonna lay you back against the seat."

Slowly, he leaned her down. Her head loped back and she closed her eyes again. "Laura, try to stay awake. Stay with me, sweetheart."

"Tired."

"I know. But I need your help."

She opened her eyes. Her pupils were dilated and she would go into shock soon. Meanwhile, the hit man might be approaching them right now.

"I need you to hold this shirt and press it against the wound. Okay. Pressure, lots of pressure. You hold on to that while I see if it's safe."

She didn't respond but she let out a moan as he

carefully shifted her head against the seat and put his jacket over her. Moving away to grab his gun, he opened his door and jumped out, taking a fast glance around the deserted road and nearby woods.

"Laura, I'm going to call Eagle Rock and then I'll make sure the shooter is gone. Eagle Rock can send the chopper to get us."

She moaned but he felt her hand move and watched as she pressed the wadded up shirt against her shoulder.

Paco looked down and saw blood covering his shirt. Laura's blood. For just a minute, he felt a buzz inside his head, could hear the drone of helicopters, the shout of soldiers, while he remembered holding a man in his arms, watching him die.

Shaking off the flashback, Paco made a vow. "I won't let you die, Laura. Do you hear me?"

She moaned again.

Hurrying, he grabbed his night vision binoculars then crouching low, moved around the wheelbase to view the damage and their location.

The truck had landed in a ditch just off the road near a big hilly pasture. They'd cut a path through the bramble and bushes, but he didn't see or hear anyone coming. Not a sound of footsteps or motors running. Whoever had shot them must have thought he'd finished the job when the truck careened off the road. Or was hiding out there, waiting to see if Paco and Laura were still alive.

Paco looked at the left back deflated tire, remembering the sound of gunshots and tires squealing. At least he'd managed to avoid hitting a tree head-on.

He had a few cuts and bruises. But Laura had been

shot. He did a quick scan with the binoculars and seeing nothing, prayed their attacker was long gone.

Grabbing his cell, he hit buttons and waited, his breath coming in great huffs, until he heard Kissie on the line. "I need help. We've been hit and Laura's injured."

"Got it," Kissie said. "Give me your coordinates."

Paco rattled off the location, remembering the nearest mile marker and the road number. "Hurry, Kissie."

"We're firing up the chopper right now. Eli and Shane will be there soon. And we'll get a doctor out here to meet y'all when you land."

Checking the area once more, Paco made sure no one was lurking in the woods. He couldn't leave the truck so he got back in and slid close to Laura, lifting her head with his hands. "How you doing?"

"I'm alive," she said, her words weak and slurred. "I want to go to sleep."

"Soon, baby, soon. Help is on the way." Frantic to keep her awake, he said, "But let's talk while we wait."

"You don't like to talk."

That was a fact but right now, nervous energy had him more than willing to spill his guts.

"I don't mind talking to you, Laura. Not now anyway."

Paco tried to make her comfortable. As long as he could hear her soft breath, he knew there was hope. So he clung to that hope as tightly as he clung to her hand in his. And then, he started talking.

"You know, up on that mountain in Afghanistan, I held a young soldier's hand just like this." He stopped, swallowed the bile of grief. "It was his first mission. He was twenty-one years old. Just starting life, Laura. So young and so confident. He died right there in my arms and there was nothing I could do for him. Nothing."

"You did your best," she said on a ragged whisper.

Shocked that he'd blurted that out, Paco prayed for the chopper to come before he said too much. But the dark night and her ragged breathing kept him talking. "They all died, Laura. All of them but me. I don't understand that."

"I know," she replied in a tightly held breath. "I know, Paco. All in your files. Can't explain. God has a plan for you."

"And what is that plan?" he said, his words harsh in the still truck. "What kind of plan allows for everyone I cared about to die and leave me like that?"

Including her? Did God intend to take Laura from him, too?

"You have more missions," she said, her words drift-ing off as her eyelids fluttered. "Important missions."

"But what about all those young men? Why didn't they get to live for one more mission? Why didn't they get to come home?"

She lifted her hand toward him then dropped it away, the look in her eyes full of longing and hope. "Look not to your own understanding...."

"Laura, Laura, don't go to sleep." He listened then let out a breath. "Laura, I hear the helicopter. Eli and Shane are here."

But Laura didn't hear him. She'd passed out.

"What's taking that doctor so long?"

Paco paced the confines of what they called the war room then turned to stare out the window, his gaze scanning the many outbuildings and fences around the secluded, sprawling compound. "We should have heard something by now."

Shane Warwick walked up to him, putting a hand on his back. "Relax, Warrior. Dr. Haines is one of the best and we have a complete medical wing in this compound. He'll do everything he can to help her and right now, he's probably thinking about what's best for Laura. She might need surgery."

Paco whirled to grab Shane's lapels. "We can't take her to a hospital. They'll come after her."

"No hospital, old boy," Shane said, gracefully lifting Paco's hands from his jacket. "We have the equipment here, if need be. And Dr. Haines served in Iraq. He knows all about triage and operating in a field hospital."

Paco stared down at his hands, realizing he'd almost attacked his best friend. "I messed up, Warwick."

Devon Malone, Brice Whelan and Eli Trudeau were all in the room. Devon stepped toward them. "You didn't mess up, Paco. You were on your way here and you did everything you could to save her."

"We were so close," Paco said, reliving the nightmare of seeing that blood flowing out of her body. "So close."

"You're here now for sure," Eli said. "You're safe, *mon ami.*"

"I don't care about being safe," Paco retorted. "I want Laura safe and healthy again. I don't get why anyone would come after that woman."

Brice shot a look at Devon. "Man, just how deep are you into this mission?"

Paco stared across at them, taking in the worried

looks on their faces. "How deep do you expect me to be?" he asked, his hands on his hips.

Brice's smile was tight-lipped. "'Consider beauty a sufficient end'," he quoted.

"And what does that mean?" Paco shot back, in the mood for a fight, not Whelan's sappy poetry.

"It's Yeats, actually," Brice said, his eyes solemn.

"I don't care who it is," Paco said. "You never make any sense, Whelan."

Eli clapped Paco on the back. "I think what this moonstruck poet is trying to say is that you're fighting for more than good over evil. You have never been one for theatrics or skittishness, Warrior. But you're obviously highly wired right now."

"Meaning?"

Devon shot Brice and Eli a warning look. "Meaning, you're either not ready for this mission or you've become emotionally involved with the subject. Or both."

Paco's pulse raged inside his body. "The *subject* is a nice woman who only wanted to help *me*. And now look at her. She's been shot!" He crossed his arms at his chest. "And as for me, I'm ready and willing since I was forced to take this on in order to protect her. We've had a couple of really bad days, so yes, I'm wired to the gill, boys. And I failed at protecting her, in spite of my best efforts. That tends to make a man skittish and *involved*."

"These people would have found her one way or another, Paco," Shane said. "They obviously want something from her. And the way I see it, she came to you at precisely the right time. If you hadn't been there to help her, she indeed might be dead already."

Kissie came into the room, followed by a young man. "Paco, this is my son, Andre. I sent Andre back to the wreck sight to look for evidence and clean things up." She turned to the tall, muscular youth. "Andre, tell them what you found."

Andre, his head shaved and his smile full of apology, handed Paco a card. "It's a business card, sir. It has Ms. Walton's information on it. Found it a few yards from where the truck landed."

Paco grabbed it. "And let me guess. It has another verse from Revelations etched invisibly on the back?"

Kissie nodded. "It does indeed. From chapter eleven, verse seven, just part of the verse: 'The beast that ascends out of the bottomless pit will make war against them, overcome them, and kill them.'"

Kissie touched Andre on the arm. "Go on back, son. Stand by and watch out for Miss Walton."

He gave Paco a shy stare then left the room.

Paco's brain buzzed with all that he'd been through and the implications of the verses he'd read. His gaze swept the room. "I think someone is declaring war on CHAIM. And they're using Laura to do it. How deep do you think I need to be into this mess now, gentlemen?"

Shane stared at the card. "We're all in it now, Warrior. In too deep to turn back."

Paco nodded. "Thank goodness I at least got Laura here alive."

Dr. Haines came into the room. "And she should stay very much alive because of your efforts."

Paco pushed toward the doctor. "How is she?"

Dr. Haines took off his glasses and cleaned them on his lab coat. "Well, she's resting now. I cleaned and debrided the wound and did a thorough search for any internal damage. Based on the X-ray, I found bullet fragments in the wound but the bullet didn't go all the way through. She probably got hit when the bullet shattered the windshield—I'd say a high-powered rifle did the job. I think I got it all, but I've given her antibiotics for infection and a pain pill to keep her quiet through the night. And I wrapped the wound to staunch the bleeding." He held up a hand. "However, if she runs a fever or presents any other signs of infection, I suggest you get her to a hospital as soon as possible."

Kissie touched Paco's arm. "I could take her into Austin and have her checked out and back in no time."

"I don't want her to leave Eagle Rock," he replied, warring with himself on how to handle this. "Doc, are you sure she's gonna be okay?"

"As long as infection doesn't set in, I think so. But again, I can't predict that. She's blessed it was a clean wound. But she'll be weak and sore for a couple of days since she got a bump on the head and she was tossed around, too."

"Can I see her?"

The doctor nodded. "Just briefly. She's exhausted and she needs to rest so her body can heal."

Sally Mae Barton entered the room, her eyes gleaming. Married to CHAIM founder Gerald Barton, Sally Mae has once worked for CHAIM. And the woman didn't pull any punches. "Mercy, let the man see her. We've dressed more wounds around here than a Civil War widow, I reckon. And we've got Selena Whelan here. She's a nurse. We'll watch over Laura, Dr. Haines. You have my word on that and we won't hold you accountable if anything does go wrong. Which it won't."

The doctor looked skeptical. But he didn't protest. "Okay then, I guess I'm done here."

"I'll show you out, Dr. Haines," Sally Mae replied with a sweet smile. Then she turned to the others. "Kissie, take Luke to see Laura. And the rest of you, get back to work on solving this case. We have a celebration coming up."

Paco looked at Kissie, hoping she'd let him stay with Laura longer than just a few minutes.

She nodded toward him. "I'll take you to her."

Devon followed them. "I'm going to check on Lydia."

Devon and Lydia had fallen in love a few years ago in spite of his secret identity and his cover as a mild-mannered minister. Now they were expecting their first child.

Paco shut his mind to the thought of bringing children into the world and concentrated instead on his work. "What next?"

Brice, Shane and Eli stood like a solid wall over the long conference table. "We'll be here," Brice said. "Hey, Dev, can you check on our ladies, too?"

Eli's wife—Devon's sister, Gena Malone Trudeau—was here with their son, Scotty. Eli had come back from the brink just to save the son he never knew he had. And he'd fallen in love with the woman raising that son.

Just one big happy family.

And that cool, calm Brit Shane Warwick had fallen for Gerald and Sally Mae's daughter, Katherine Atkins. They'd gotten married in England but planned a second service in the spring here in Texas.

Devon smiled at Brice's request. "Of course. I'm sure they're not happy about this lockdown we're under now."

"Better safe than sorry," Eli said, his tone grim.

Paco gave them all one last look, his heart twisted with feelings he didn't want to explore right now, then followed Kissie to another wing of the house.

As they snaked through hallways and doors that required scanners and key cards in order to unlock, he asked, "Is she being guarded?"

"She is," Kissie replied. "Andre volunteered for the first shift."

"I'll take a shift, too," Paco replied.

Because he wasn't going anywhere until he knew Laura was going to pull out of this. And once he was sure she was safe and well, he was going to find Lawrence Henner and have a long talk with the man.

If talking didn't work, Paco would go into action mode and get the truth, no matter what.

He had a new mission now.

And if God had brought him to this mission then Paco aimed to finish it to the bitter end. For Laura's sake.

FIFTEEN

Paco entered the sterile room hidden in the back of the big, rambling complex, nodding to Andre as he opened the door. Lydia Malone smiled up at him. She sat next to Laura's bed, reading what looked like a devotional book.

"Luke," she said, struggling to get up. Pregnancy agreed with the pretty blond-haired woman. In spite of her rounded stomach, she was glowing, her soft smile full of understanding and compassion.

"Hello, Lydia." He didn't waste time with the niceties. He went straight to the bed and took Laura's hand. She was as pale as the crisp white sheet and blanket covering her. "How is she?"

Lydia came to stand beside him. "I think she's gonna be just fine. She's sleeping now. The doctor gave her something to help her relax and the antibiotics are probably making her drowsy, too." Then she glanced at him. "How're you doing?"

Paco found it hard to look into Lydia's vivid, all-knowing eyes. The woman had a direct link to the Almighty and she used it with all the precision of a hunter with a bow. "I've been better."

Lydia nodded then touched a hand to her stomach. "I've prayed for both of you."

"I have no doubt of that," he replied. "Thank you."

Lydia looked down at Laura. "She was asking for you earlier."

His heart did a funny little thing that made him think of a tank roaring across rocks. "She was?"

Lydia looked from Laura's pale face back to him, a silent stealth message passing between them. "Talk to her. It might help her."

He nodded, the knot in his throat choking him with misery. "I'm not good at talking."

"You don't have to be good at it," Lydia replied. "Just speak with honesty. Laura, like most women, probably values honesty above all else."

Paco stood silent as Lydia discreetly left the room. How could he be honest with this sweet woman? How could he tell her that he wasn't worth her trouble? That he *was* trouble.

He went to the door. "Andre, you can go now. I'll take the next shift."

"Yes, sir." Andre's big brown eyes held a thousand questions. None of which Paco wanted to answer right now. He wasn't a hero and he didn't want the kid staring at him with admiration or anticipation. But he didn't want to discourage the kid either. Andre was about to become a man and life was hard. That was all Paco could really tell him.

But he couldn't talk to the kid right now. He only wanted to sit here with Laura and will her to wake up and fuss at him. It was pretty amazing that he'd only known her for a few days and yet, she'd come bursting into his life full of fire and determination and just like that, she'd changed him. He wished they could have met under different circumstances but then he probably would have pushed her away. Even on a good day, he was so good at alienating anyone who cared about him.

But just knowing that she'd cared enough to find him based on a desperate midnight call, touched Paco deep inside his burned, battered, scarred heart.

And scared him more than anything he'd ever encountered.

So he sat down in the middle of the night and he talked in soft tones to the woman sleeping in the bed. He took her hand and he told her all about the horrors of being trapped on that mountain, the agony of watching his men die, and the relief that he hated each time he took another breath. He told her about the dreams and how they'd come all during the night. About how, in the dreams, he was left standing in a white-hot desert, the silence so telling it made him want to scream out in agony, the intense loneliness he experienced so bitter and cutting, he felt as if he truly was the last man left on earth.

He told her about when he was young and how his family had struggled, so Paco decided to follow in the family tradition and join the military to see the world and learn more about life. Then after his first tour, he was asked to join CHAIM. And even though he re-upped with the military, he did join CHAIM because he wanted to fight the good fight and be a good man like his own father—the father he'd never really known. He also wanted to honor God, both on and off the battlefield.

But he'd done so many things that didn't honor God. And he's seen so much that didn't honor God. He'd felt thoughts that didn't honor God. So why would God honor any of his prayers now?

"I shouldn't be here, Laura. I don't have any right to be here."

When he tired of talking, he stopped to pray, leaning forward so that his forehead touched her hand, his prayers asking for some of her softness, for some of her strength and integrity and faith. She has such soft, pretty hands. So soft and so pretty that he yanked his calloused, scarred fingers away for fear he'd damage her in some way.

By the time he was finished, the sun was rising toward the east and he could hear birds chirping just outside the high, secure windows.

The room became flooded with a brilliant creamy yellow glow that hurt Paco's tired eyes. The silence of that light sent shivers down his spine but he could still hear the birds fussing and playing in the courtyard. How he wished he could see God's touch in that brilliant light, hear the Lord's words in the song of the birds.

Then he heard *her.* He heard Laura's gentle voice.

"*I'm* glad you're here, Paco. You're not on that mountain alone now. You have God and you have me."

And right then and there, Luke Paco Martinez knew God had brought him to this very moment, the moment when he'd accepted God back into his heart and the moment when he'd finally fallen in love.

Laura tried to smile but the effort hurt too much. Paco reached for her hand, his gaze holding her in a tender way that seemed different from his usual cynical, abrupt nature. She'd heard his confession, her mind drifting between sleep and being awake. She'd wondered at times if she was just in a long dream where he trusted her and wanted to talk to her. At other times, she knew she was fully coherent and this troubled, honorable man was pouring his heart out to her because he thought she was asleep. So she didn't speak and she didn't dare move and she ignored the creeping pain in her body to listen to his quiet voice.

That voice had carried her through till morning.

That and her silent prayers to God each time Paco let go of another nightmare memory.

"Hi," she said, remembering his hands covering hers, his head bowed near her. Did he know she'd prayed right along with him?

"Hi." He didn't say anything else. He didn't have to. And she didn't have to tell him that she'd heard him off and on during the long night, his words blurring out the pain ebbing and flowing with each heartbeat. Laura had focused on his monotone words, her heart aching in a different way than her bones and tissue.

So now, she stared up at him while she thanked God for allowing her to find Paco Martinez. *Lord, this good man is hurting. He needs Your love now more than ever. I don't know why he lived when others died, but I do know You hold all the answers. I'm willing to trust all of that to You, if You'll trust me with him.*

"I'm okay," she told Paco. "You don't need to worry about me."

He nodded, his hand tight over hers. "I have to finish what we started, sweetheart."

"I know. I don't want you to and I don't understand why these people are coming after me, but I understand why you need to do this."

He opened his mouth to say something else, but the

door swung open and Eli Trudeau stepped in. "Sorry, Paco, but we need you in the war room."

Laura didn't miss the urgency in his words or the hesitation his expression held when he glanced toward her.

Paco reluctantly let go of her hand then nodded. Looking down at her, he said "I'll be back soon. Rest."

Laura gave him a weak thumbs-up.

Then Sally Mae and Selena entered the room and started fussing over her, so she didn't get a chance to tell him goodbye.

"What is it?" Paco asked as he hurried up the long hallway with Eli, both waiting as the scanners and ID cards gave them access to the next wing.

"Bad stuff, man," Eli said, glancing around. "A report of a dead body out near where you ran off the road."

"And?"

"And the body was identified by some of the locals. Kissie got a hit on the report just minutes ago. It's the same MO, Paco. Shooter was Kevin Booker from Flagstaff, Arizona. Worked for CHAIM for a year as an officer manager who mainly served as a liaison between field agents and supervisors. Was fired three months ago for giving out highly sensitive information to certain factions."

Paco let out a tired sigh. "Was he a former patient of Laura's?"

Eli shot him a hard stare. "Bingo. Saw her right after he lost his job."

They'd reached the door to the conference room.

Eli stepped aside and let Paco go ahead of him.

The big room was full to the brim with CHAIM people.

Starting with the team and ending with the founding members—Gerald Barton, John Simpson and Alfred Anderson. And the father of Brice's wife Selena, Delton Carter.

They were all staring at Paco.

"I'm Selena," the golden-haired nurse told Laura as she checked her vitals and readjusted the drip bag. "I helped Dr. Haines clean and treat your wound last night."

"You're Brice's wife, right?" Laura asked, her voice sounding hollow and raw to her ears.

Selena nodded then smiled. "Yes, for about six months now."

"You went through your own ordeal."

Selena nodded. "I sure did. I have an idea how you might feel, being chased by people you tried to help. The doctor I worked for was corrupt and I almost let him get away with it out of respect and fear. Won't make that mistake again."

Laura took a breath then grimaced as pain shot through her. "Sometimes we do things for all the wrong reasons, thinking we're doing them for the right reasons."

"Exactly." Selena finished her work then patted Laura's arm. "You didn't cause this, Laura. Someone somewhere wants to come after all of us. And he would have done it, with or without you."

"But why me?" Laura asked, sick with frustration. "Why me and why now?"

"He was probably waiting for the perfect time to

strike," Selena said. "My father thinks this person wants a lot of power and he's trying to obtain it through CHAIM."

"But we're all here now," Laura said. "How can he hurt anyone else?"

Selena didn't answer. But Laura saw the apprehension moving through Selena's blue eyes. And felt that same apprehension building inside her booming heart.

"You don't think…"

Selena shook her head. "The entire team is working on this, including my father and the other founding members. You need to rest right now. Try not to think about all of this."

After asking if she needed anything else, Selena left the room. But Laura couldn't rest. Not when it seemed as if she'd be putting everyone here in danger just by being at Eagle Rock. Paco had believed this to be the safest place for her right now.

But what if it wasn't?

Paco held his stance, his expression never changing. He knew all about Eagle Rock. Agents were brought here for training, for fellowship and workshops, and for reprimands. He figured he was about to get the latter, big time.

"Talk to me, gentlemen," he said. "Let me have it. All of it."

Shane stepped forward. "We have a theory, Paco."

"I'm listening."

Gerald Barton motioned to the conference table. "Let's sit down. We might be here a while."

"What about Laura?" Paco asked, looking at the door.

"Selena is with her and Andre's back guarding her door," Gerald replied.

Paco didn't miss the look passing amongst the men. He needed to get his head back on straight and focus on this mission. He sat down and waited.

Delton Carter nodded toward Shane. "Go ahead, Warwick."

Shane went to the big board on one wall. "We've established a connection to Laura Walton with each of the three men who've come after her—Howard Barrow at the café, John Rutherford in the desert and Kevin Booker out on the road last night. They were all former patients of Laura's and they all currently worked for CSN—Central Security Network, which happens to be owned by one Lawrence Henner. They each also either tried to work for CHAIM or have worked for CHAIM briefly at various times.

"Lawrence Henner's son Kyle was also a patient of Laura Walton's. Sixteen years old. He committed suicide a few months ago. Meantime, Laura dated Alex Whitmyer but when things became uncomfortable for her, she broke it off and had to get a restraining order when Whitmyer started stalking her. And Whitmyer also works for Lawrence Henner.

"So we have this connection between Laura Walton and Lawrence Henner…and CHAIM."

Shane stopped, letting that statement soak in.

Brice got up and took over.

"Three of the above mentioned men are dead now— Barrows shot by Laura at the café, Rutherford killed by Paco in the desert and the third one—Booker—killed by someone else out on the road last night."

"Which means whoever is doing this means business," Brice said. "He killed his own man last night—"

"Because that man failed," Paco finished. "Shane, that's what happened this summer with you and Katherine. They killed their own people to keep 'em silent."

"We've noted that similarity," Shane replied. "But the people responsible for that are accounted for and serving jail time now. We can't trace anything back to that incident."

Devon leaned forward. "We don't know yet who killed Kevin Booker, Paco. But we'll find out. The point is—it's all connected to Henner and it's all connected to Laura."

"Which brings us to our theory—because they're all also connected to CHAIM. We believe you're right— Henner is coming after CHAIM and he used Laura to do it. And you brought her here to protect her, thus exposing all of us to this danger."

The implication of that statement hit Paco with lightning swift clarity. "You're not thinking—"

Gerald Barton lifted a hand. "We have to consider every angle, Warrior. We could all very well be in danger, but we can't be sure at this point. But, son, it doesn't look good."

Paco stood up. "You keep working on all the angles, but I'm going after Lawrence Henner. The man hired all of these people to do his dirty work—we have that connection, too, right?"

"You're right, bro," Eli said. "Henner hired all three men to work at Central Security Network. And we have the other connection."

"They all worked for CHAIM at one time or another," Paco finished. "And failed."

"And that's the sticking point," Eli replied.

Shane pointed to the names. "Barrow, Rutherford and Booker were not CHAIM material. And let's be honest here, based on their clumsy attempts to harm Laura, they weren't trained operatives under CSN, either. So the big question is why would Lawrence Henner hire men he knew would fail?"

"And why did he come after Laura?" Paco asked, that question foremost in his mind. "She thinks he blames her for his son's death but it sounds like the man himself might be responsible."

"We have a theory on that, too," Shane replied. "We think he was watching Laura, maybe had someone on the inside keeping tabs on her work, her whereabouts. He was just waiting—"

"For her to come to me?" Paco asked, jumping up. "Warwick, are you saying all of this was to get to me?"

"We think maybe he waited to get to one of us, yes," Shane said. "But there's more. As we said, we also believe he's not only targeting you and Laura. He wants to come after all of CHAIM, taking us out one by one. When Laura found you, he went into action."

"But why?" Paco asked, his mind whirling.

Gerald Barton stood up and glanced around the room. "We believe he's trying to form his own undercover team. But we also believe his team will be much different from ours. Lawrence Henner is forming a vigilante group."

"For what purpose?" Paco asked, his heart aching with apprehension and concern. And rage.

"That's what we have to figure out," Shane said. "And it will take all of us working together to do so."

SIXTEEN

Paco wasn't so sure about that together part. But he had promised Laura he'd ask for help. Could he do that?

Devon shifted in his chair. "You can't do this alone, Paco. We won't let you."

"You won't let me?" Paco took his dear sweet time eyeing each of them. They'd all been together for years, so it was only natural that they could read each other so easily. "Is this some sort of intervention?"

Eli huffed a chuckle. "*Non,* bro. It's not like that. Listen to one who knows—this is bigger than you. Now, you can be a hotshot and take off like a lone wolf into the wild or you can let this team—*your team*—help you out."

Paco sank down on a chair, his mind whirling with what he could do and what he should do. Were they right about this? Laura had seen this coming and she'd only known him a few days. These men knew his soul and his flaws. But did he dare reach out for help? Wasn't that a sign of weakness?

"There's no shame in having a team to back you," Devon said. "Especially now when we could all be in danger."

Paco looked up at Devon. "Do you think Henner will come after us here?"

"It could happen," Devon said. "In spite of our precautions and our security measures, if someone wants to get to us badly enough, they can find a way. Especially someone who also runs a security company."

Paco couldn't let that happen. "I brought Laura here to protect her. Maybe that's what Henner expected and wanted since we think he's in the vicinity."

"That's all the more reason to do some recon, old boy," Warwick said with an eloquent shrug.

But Paco saw the shade of worry in Warwick's cold-steel eyes. He couldn't let these men down. And he wouldn't put their loves ones—or Laura—in harm's way. Maybe if he hadn't been so determined to win at all costs on that mountainside in the Middle East, his men might be alive today. And maybe Laura was right. Maybe God did have one more mission in mind for Paco Martinez.

"All right," he said, tapping his hands on the table. "I need help on this. Where do we start?"

Warwick nodded his approval, admiration in his eyes. "We start at the beginning, going back over everything. But first, we decide who goes out there with you and who stays here to protect everyone else."

The founding members argued amongst themselves and finally all agreed they were too old to do field work, so they'd stay here and monitor the situation.

"With the women and children," Gerald said with a cowboy twang. "Just like the good old days even if we can't go out into the fray."

"Your wife would tell you she can handle that part," Delton Carter said with a smile.

"She probably could," Gerald agreed. "But I ain't going anywhere. Time for these young cowboys to take over."

Shane looked at Devon. "Dev, you should stay here with Lydia."

Paco watched Devon's face, saw the battle of duty toward CHAIM warring with duty toward his wife and unborn child. "I don't think—"

"Then I'll think for you, bro," Eli said. "Do not leave her and that babe here alone. Trust me, it's not worth it."

Eli should know, Paco thought. He'd gone on a mission only to return to find his pregnant wife had been taken. He believed she'd died but she'd survived in a coma long enough for her child to be born. And Devon had protected that child from everyone, even an unstable Eli, up until a year or so ago.

Devon shot Eli a long look. "You're right. Gena won't like it if you go and I stay, but I can watch over Scotty for you if I stay behind."

"Just as you did before," Eli reminded him.

Brice stepped forward. "I'm more than willing to go out with you, Paco."

Delton Carter shook his head. "Brice, I'd feel better if you stayed here to help Kissie with the technical details. And besides, you're good with hostage situations and interrogation."

Brice frowned then nodded. "Just in case?"

"Just in case," Delton replied, his expression grim.

Warwick glanced around the room. "So it's settled. Paco, Eli and I will try to track down Lawrence Henner, first to observe and report, then to get proof of what we think he's trying to do. If we find proof, we call in the authorities and make sure we stop this before anyone else gets hurt."

Paco got up. "That just leaves one detail. Who's going to tell the women about this?"

Laura had expected him to come back. She looked up when Paco walked through the door to her room, her heart jolting her pulse into a heavy cadence she could feel beating against her temple.

"Hi," she said, trying to smile.

"Hi," he replied back, without a smile.

"You're going after him, aren't you?"

He didn't even seem surprised at her words. "I have to. We've connected some of the dots and—"

"And Lawrence Henner has several people working for him, people who tried to or either became CHAIM agents but wound up being my patients, not to mention my stalker ex-boyfriend, who also works for Henner. And Mr. Henner is bitter about his son's suicide. Something else I was involved in. Did I miss any of the dots?"

He almost smiled at that. "No. You've pretty much put it all together. But, we also hit on something else, sweetheart. Something you said early on."

She shifted, grimaced with pain. "What?"

"Me," he replied. "We're beginning to think he used you to get to me, somehow. If he wanted either of us dead, we'd be gone by now. But he knew I'd protect you."

She shook her head. "That can't be. Henner had no idea you'd call me that night or that I'd go out and try to find you."

"But he could have pinned his hopes on you becoming

my counselor sooner or later. We gave him the sooner the night I called you. He could have been waiting for a CHAIM operative to call for help. And I guess I got the short straw."

"Do you think he tapped the hotline?"

"Wouldn't put it past him. Especially if he wanted to monitor the whereabouts of what people consider an unstable CHAIM agent. He obviously did his homework on that one."

Realization colored her expression. "It does seem each CSN person he sent after us was unstable, doesn't it? Surely he doesn't think you'd turn on CHAIM and join up with him?"

He shrugged, looking uncomfortable. "Hard to rationalize a madman's plan. Everyone thinks I'm on the brink. Why not Henner, too?"

"You're not like those men, Paco."

He stood there, looking down at her for a long minute then he reached out and took her hand, his gaze dancing around the room. "I talked to you last night. I told you everything."

"I know," she said, watching for his reaction.

His gaze slammed into hers. "You heard me?"

"I heard most of it." She smiled. "I heard what God wanted me to hear, I think."

He let go of her hand and backed away. "I thought—"

"You thought no one was listening." Laura reached out for him again. "Paco, you have to remember something about God and me. When it comes to you, we're both willing to listen."

His expression went from hard-edged and unyielding

to open-faced disbelief and finally, a quiet awe. "Why me, Laura?"

"Why not you, Paco?" She held tightly to the edge of her blanket. "Maybe the only way you could truly confide in someone was exactly the way it happened, while you thought no one was listening. But I heard you and I'm telling you, we can get you through this. You have to forgive yourself and you have to let go. But that's easier said than done. I should listen to my own advice."

He took her hand back in his. "You amaze me, you know."

Laura felt the heat of that gentle praise warming her all the way to her toes. "I take my job very seriously," she said to hide that heat.

"So do I," he retorted. "And I want the world—your world—to be safe again."

That shattered the delicate emotions floating like crystal inside her head. "So you have to finish this, right?"

"Right. Henner's either after me or he wants to bring down CHAIM."

"Why would he do that?"

"Power, vengeance, greed. Your guess is as good as mine, sweetheart." He leaned down close. "But I intend to find out."

Laura stared up at him, her heart hammering so fast she thought it might burst out of her chest. "Could you do me one favor before you leave me?"

He leaned in a little farther, his dark eyes burning with a brilliant fire. "Anything."

"Kiss me goodbye."

The look on his face wasn't very encouraging. Laura's

warmth turned to an outright blush of shame. She turned her head away, mortified. "I'm sorry. Just go."

The next thing she knew, Paco was lifting her head back around, his hands pulling through her tangled hair as he lowered his head to hers. The kiss started out as a fast and furious peck and ended up as a slow and caressing, very real kiss.

This is how it is with us, Laura thought as her mind filled with the essence of Paco Martinez. This is how it will be with us. This guessing, wishing, needing, finding.

She didn't want it to end.

But he pulled away just as quickly as he'd come close.

"You didn't have to give me a mercy kiss," she said, tears forming in her eyes in spite of her intake of breath.

He touched a hand back to her hair, his eyes locking with hers. "Sweetheart, that was not a mercy kiss. That was a promise that I don't have the right to make to you."

Hope lifted her. "What kind of promise, Paco?"

He kissed her again, his lips feathering over her tears. "A promise that I will be back. For you."

And then, he was gone, just like that, the imprint of his hard-edged touch and his hard-fought promise lingering like a distant mountain vista just beyond her mind.

Paco did one last check of the wing where Laura was recovering, making sure Andre was standing guard and Devon and Brice would take shifts, too. Selena had assured him all of Laura's vitals were good and she had no signs of fever or infection. Dr. Haines was scheduled to return later to check on her again, but Paco trusted Selena until then.

Brice met him outside the secure wing. "Things are about as tight as we can get them, Warrior. You have my word I'll take care of everyone here."

"Laura," Paco replied, the memories of her satin-sweet touch lingering in his mind. "I need you to protect Laura."

"Granted," Brice replied, his expression questioning.

Paco wasn't ready to answer any questions right now. These new feelings were too bittersweet with their intensity and too raw and fresh for him to make any kind of declarations. He'd get through this task and then he'd step back and examine these new sensations rushing through him like a gully-wash over a dry creek bed.

"You okay, friend?" Brice asked as they headed back toward the war room.

"As okay as a man can be," Paco replied.

Kissie and Eli met them at the door. "I've isolated the signal from Laura's laptop," Kissie said.

"Where?" Paco asked.

"Just as we thought," Eli replied. "The laptop is at Lawrence Henner's estate about an hour outside of Austin."

She gave them the coordinates. "He doesn't know we're onto him."

"Or he wants us to find him," Eli warned.

"Either way, I'm gonna pay the man a visit," Paco retorted.

"And Shane and I are going with you," Eli countered.

Paco saw Shane coming up the hall. "Gear's all packed. Ready, gentlemen?"

Eli nodded. "I've explained to Gena and she's good. Well, as good as Gena can be—stubborn woman that she is. And Scotty's mad he can't go with us."

Shane's grin didn't reach his eyes. "Same here. Katherine is with her mother, putting on a brave front. No, that's not quite true. She is brave, very brave." He frowned. "Too brave. I'll have to remind Brice of that."

They both looked at Paco. "How's Laura?" Shane asked.

"Laura knew this was coming," Paco said, rather than getting all sappy like these two lovesick cods. "Let's get out of here."

He saw the lift of Kissie's dark eyebrows but thankfully, she didn't say anything. Except her call as they went down the hallway.

"Stay safe. You have my prayers."

They all needed that, Paco decided. And inside his head, no, inside his heart, he felt that same tug that his buddies must be feeling. He didn't want to leave Laura.

But he had to do this in order to come back to her, whole and healed and ready to kiss her one more time.

Laura had visitors in the hours after Paco, Eli and Shane left. She figured these strong, supportive women were not only trying to distract and comfort her, but were also trying to keep themselves centered and calm, too. They had to be used to this kind of scene where their loved ones left to save the world, but she sure wasn't.

Now several women huddled around her bedchamber, some sitting on the edge of her bed and some settled into the comfortable chairs that had appeared in her room.

"This reminds me of that scene in *Gone With the Wind*," Lydia, a Georgia girl, said with a drawl. "You know when the men go out to protect Scarlett's honor after she was accosted near her mill by Shantytown. They're all sitting around knitting and stitching, their nerves on edge, while their men are out there about to get in a big fight."

"I've never seen that movie," dark-haired Gena Malone Trudeau said. "And I don't knit. I'm sure my nerves will be shot before this is over. At least Brice is entertaining Scotty for me."

"You should read the book," Selena, also born and raised in Georgia, replied as she filled Laura's water glass. "It's better than the movie. Brice has read it several times to 'understand the southern female mindset,' or so he tells me. That's my Irish poet, always trying to maintain his sensitive side."

"I've practically memorized it," Lydia replied with a smile. "My favorite book ever. I have the movie poster in our bedroom even though Devon frowns every time he walks by it."

Katherine Barton Warwick, the cool Texas blonde now married to Shane Warwick, patted her smooth bob, her gaze moving over Laura. "How do you feel?"

Laura looked up in surprise. "About *Gone With the Wind?* I can take it or leave it."

They all laughed. "She's asking how *you* feel," Selena said with an indulging smile. "Are you in pain? Do you want us to leave so you can rest better?"

"I'm fine," Laura said. "Just sore. And no, I don't

want you to leave. I can't rest. But y'all have taken good care of me. I appreciate that."

"I made mother and the others go to their rooms," Katherine replied. "She has a tendency to hover. They all love it when we're gathered here. They try to spoil us."

"Your mother is nice," Laura said, wondering how she could keep this constant fear at bay. "And scary at times, too."

"She is one of the strongest women I've ever met," Selena replied. "And so are her friends, Mrs. Simpson and Mrs. Anderson, and my own mother, for that matter. In fact, we're all pretty amazing." She grinned then winked at Laura. "It's nice to have a circle of friends to get us through the stress of being involved with men who work in such high-risk jobs."

"How do you do that?" Laura asked. "How do women live with sending their men into battle?"

Katherine shook her head. "There are all kinds of battles out there and our husbands fight them each and every day. All men have battles to fight, whether they work for some sort of secret organization or they work at the local bank or grocery store. It's part of life. And yes, it takes some adjustment, trying to make it balance. And trying to understand it."

"It's hard," Selena said. "But we have to trust in God and in those we love. It took me a long time to figure that out."

The silence and the glances passing between the four other women forced Laura to ask her next question. "What if the one you love is trying hard not to love you back?"

Selena leaned forward. "Oh, we all have a story to tell about that, don't we, girls?"

"Oh, yes," Gena said, shaking her head. "That's something I do know a lot about—even though I lived in isolation in Maine most of my adult years."

"I've got some time on my hands," Laura replied. "And I'd really like to hear all of your stories."

Lydia held up her hand. "It all started with Pastor Dev and me…and you won't believe what happened."

He couldn't believe this.

Paco stood with Shane and Eli inside a big, cozy den centered in the massive hill country hunting lodge owned by Lawrence Henner. Stood and looked at Laura's laptop sitting on a pristine oak desk nestled by the big bay window of the grand room.

"He's not here," Eli said, stating the obvious.

"But the laptop is, of course," Paco replied while he searched the desk drawers. And found nothing much to help them. Hitting a hand on the desk, he said, "I don't get the man. He leaves clues and a wide-open trail. What's he trying to prove?"

They'd searched the whole house and that covered a lot of square feet in this creepy, dark, depressing place. Lawrence Henner wasn't here. In fact, no one was here.

Paco touched the mouse pad on the laptop and the screen came to life. "Look, another scripture passage. Revelations Six, Verse Two: 'And I looked, and behold, a white horse. And he who sat on it had a bow; and a crown was given to him, and he went out conquering and to conquer.'"

"We saw a white horse out in the pasture here," Shane

said on a low whisper. Then he put a hand on the leather chair behind the desk. "Obviously, he *did* know we were on to him and he set us up. Seems he's also setting himself up to be some sort of hero."

Paco whirled, headed for the door. "Yeah, which means he could be on his way to Eagle Rock right now."

Shane grabbed the laptop then hurried to follow Paco and Eli. They made it out into the hallway.

Then Paco heard a chuckle coming from the dark shadows on the other side of the wide planked hall.

"Finally, some company. I was getting downright lonely, waiting for the famous Paco Martinez to come and visit. What a bonus that you have most of the CHAIM team with you, too."

"Henner?" Paco said, his gun drawn.

"Not even close," the voice replied.

Then a man stepped out of the shadows, his own gun raised toward Paco and the others. "I suggest you lower your weapons, gentlemen. You're surrounded, even if we didn't extend a nice welcome when you broke in—I mean—arrived earlier."

"Who are you?" Shane asked, his tone conversational and almost light-hearted.

The slender blond-haired man stepped even closer. "Me? I'm Laura's heartbroken boyfriend—the one she put a restraining order on. I'm Alex Whitmyer. And I've been waiting a long time to meet all of you. Now, tell me, how's my dear sweet Laura doing these days?"

SEVENTEEN

Late afternoon sunshine filtered through the windows of Laura's room. All of the women had left except Lydia. She was in the comfortable blue armchair by the bed, reading out loud to Laura from a humorous devotional book.

Laura laughed as Lydia finished yet another comical story with an inspirational point. "Thank you," she said. "I appreciate everyone sharing your stories. It's so amazing how you all met CHAIM agents and fell in love."

"Add one more to that list," Lydia said, patting her rounded tummy. "Paco was the last holdout."

"He might still be the last holdout," Laura replied, wondering where he was right now. "I wish we'd hear something."

Lydia shook her head. "They only tell us things on a need-to-know basis. I'm sure Brice and Devon are getting hourly updates."

"Eagle Rock does make me feel safe," Laura said, hoping to hold off the sense of dread coursing through her heart. "I wonder what will happen between Paco and me, when this is over."

Lydia looked down at her book. "He still has a lot of healing to do. I'd be cautious if I were you."

"I've always been that," Laura said, glancing at the clock. "But my one mistake has come back to haunt me. Alex Whitmyer. I think he's involved in this whole mess."

"He's on the radar screen," Lydia said. "I've heard his name mentioned but no one can locate him."

And that was the source of Laura's dread.

They heard footsteps outside then the door opened.

"Dr. Haines," Lydia said, getting up. "We thought you'd be here at noon."

The doctor looked haggard, his eyes rimmed with fatigue, a frown pulling on his face. "I…uh…had a conflict."

"Well, you're here now," Lydia said. "I'll get Selena so you can examine Laura."

Another man stepped around the door behind Dr. Haines. "That won't be necessary, Mrs. Malone. No one will be examining Laura Walton today."

Laura gasped, her worst fears shining inside the man's demented eyes.

Lydia glanced from the man to Laura, realization coloring her skin. "Who are you?"

Laura reached out toward Lydia. "He's the man we were just talking about. Lydia, this is Alex Whitmyer."

Alex grinned. "The stalker ex-boyfriend, come to fetch little Laura home."

He hurt all over, but Paco was alive. And mad.

And sitting in some dark smelly dungeon.

"Paco?"

Shane's voice was like a hollow echo.

"I'm here. What's left of me, that is."

"Eli?"

"*Oui*, John-boy," Eli retorted with a snarl. "Enough with the roll call. We need to get out of here."

"Got a plan, old boy?" Shane asked, his tone now back to drawing room pitch.

Paco grunted against the ropes holding his arms and legs tied. "He didn't gag us. His mistake. We can scream, at least."

"No need to silence us," Shane said. "Who would hear us out here on this lonely stretch of land?"

"Why didn't he kill us?" Eli asked, the echo of his surprise hitting the rafters. "I reckon beating us to a pulp was a bit more fun for him."

"He wants us alive, remember?" Paco replied. "The man actually thinks he can form his own vigilante team. But if he's trying to convince us to join up, this wasn't the smartest way to do it."

"Not with us," Eli said. "He might think he can brainwash us into becoming his puppets, or maybe he plans to drug us to the point we'll do anything he says. Apparently, he tried to do that with the other poor saps. Ain't gonna happen. Not as long as I have breath in my body."

Paco heard Shane moving around. "While we're figuring out how the man managed to hide a whole half dozen men and how those men managed to overpower us and dump us here, let's also figure out how to get out of here."

"To get back to Eagle Rock," Paco said, his fingers twisting against the ropes. "He wants Laura. We thought Henner was behind this but all along it's been Whitmyer."

"I fear Henner is long dead," Shane said, a grunt of exertion coloring his words. "And probably buried somewhere here on his own property. Whitmyer has obviously taken his place. Wonder how that'll go over at the Christmas party?"

"He's gone not only rogue, but psycho-rogue," Eli said on a snort. "The worst kind. I feel better about my past bad habits now, for true."

"Enough chitchat," Shane said, the rustling of ropes around him. "We need to move on while we can still stand."

Paco let out one last grunt as he managed to tug at the circle of knots around his wrist. "I'm out," he said, quickly untying his feet.

"Me, too," Shane replied, his grin flashing in the dark, dank room.

"Eli?"

Paco felt a nudge from behind. "What are we waiting for?" Eli asked. "Whitmyer might have Henner's white horse, but we have something else on our side."

"What's that?" Paco asked.

"People we love," Eli replied. "And that can make a man mean with honor, understand?"

"I hear that," Paco said. Because sitting here in this gloomy cold basement had brought a clear light to his eyes.

He loved Laura.

And he was going back to her, just as he'd promised.

Please, Lord, don't let me be too late.

* * *

She wasn't going to let this happen.

Laura looked at the man holding a gun on Dr. Haines.

"How did you get in, Alex?"

His glassy gaze held her. "Well, it wasn't easy, little darling, that's for sure. First, I had to take your laptop so I could scan all the files and find some vital passwords and information. Then I had figure out where that brooding has-been soldier was taking you and get the right people to follow you. Only, that didn't work out the way I'd planned." He let out an exaggerated sigh. "And then, I had to wait until I could find a way in the back door to this fort. A few security codes jammed and changed and the doctor was more than happy to oblige—"

"He threatened my wife," Dr. Haines said, pointing a finger at Alex. "And he knocked out that young man out there and moved him to another part of the building. Held a gun on me while I tied him up. He's—"

"Shut up," Whitmyer said, poking at the doctor with his gun. "We're here now but if you keep whining, old man, I can put you out of your misery. And *then* go after your wife. So I suggest you don't say a word, not about what I've done with that kid or anything else you've seen here."

The doctor's shocked silence ended that conversation.

Laura tried to reason with him. "You might have us locked inside this room, Alex, but there are others here." She saw Lydia's warning glance. "There is an agent on sight."

"Oh, you mean a powerful CHAIM agent? Right. I

get that, Laura. I came prepared, of course. They won't bother us." He pointed the gun toward Lydia. "Not if they want little mama here to live."

Laura glanced at Lydia. Whitmyer had forced Lydia back in her chair. They were trapped in this room with a madman and a shaking doctor. And she had no idea where Andre was. Or Brice, Devon and the others for that matter. So she did the best thing she could do. She went into therapist mode, hoping her questions would distract him.

"Did you hire those men to come after me?"

Alex grinned. "Oh, you mean those losers who wanted to be super agents? Yeah, I kind of set them up. I told them if they'd prove themselves I'd let them join one of Henner's special teams." He laughed. "I learned a lot of inside information, dating you. Found out so many fascinating things from hacking into your files, too. Those wannabes fell for it and did precisely what I thought they'd do. They messed up. Oops. But hey, got everyone's attention, didn't it?"

He laughed, glancing over to where Dr. Haines sat patting Lydia's arm more to calm himself than Lydia, Laura thought, her heart going out to the doctor.

"Where is Mr. Henner?" Lydia asked, her tone calm and guarded, a fierce determination in her eyes.

Whitmyer shook his head. "Out of the country for a while."

"Did you hurt Kyle's father?" Laura shouted. "Alex, why would you do that? Why are you doing any of this?"

"The old man was depressed," he retorted with a shrug. "He'd lost focus on our plans. I had to do something to save the company, to save his empire. And to prove to you that I'm worthy, of course."

"It wasn't your place to do that," Laura said, her prayers bringing calm over her now that she saw him face-to-face and knew he was behind all of this. Maybe she could talk him through this. "And you don't have to prove anything to me."

But Alex wasn't having any of that. "It was my place. I worked hard for that man for years, jumping like a dog every time he wanted things done. And he never saw it. He wanted his stupid son to man up and get with the program. Why? He had me right there all the time. I tried to show him we could take his company to the next level. But after you messed things up and his weak son offed himself, Henner went from blaming you to blaming himself. He wouldn't listen to reason so I had to act fast."

"Is that why you dated me?" Laura asked, stalling, praying Brice, Devon and Kissie would figure things out.

He pushed off the locked door. "No, no. I dated you because I loved you…and I needed access to your file of reject-CHAIM agents and crazy rogue agents. I had this grand plan to take you with me into CSN, to create an organization better than CHAIM. After reading your files, I figured that whacked-out Martinez would jump at the chance. So when I heard you were going to find him, I set things into motion. And here we are."

"There is no better organization than CHAIM," Lydia said, rising off her chair. "And you need to understand what a mistake you've made here today."

Whitmyer pushed the gun at her. "Sit down. The only

mistake I made was wasting my time with Martinez and his merry band of followers."

"You've seen Paco?" Laura tried to sit up straight. It was hard to breathe. And her calm was fast disappearing.

Whitmyer shot her a cold stare. "Saw him, made him an offer—which he refused—and then made sure none of them will be returning here tonight."

Laura gasped. "What did you do to them?"

Whitmyer walked over to her bed. "Ah, now, I never heard you worry like that for me. What happened? You go and fall for that worthless burned out soldier?"

Laura swallowed a retort, her mind centered on the one hope that Paco and the others were still alive. "I was trying to help him when all of this started."

"Yeah, I saw some of those tender moments," Whitmyer replied, his face inches from hers. "You've betrayed me, Laura. Just like everyone else I depended on."

"So why are you here then?" she asked, anger giving her strength. "Why didn't you kill me yourself, instead of sending those men? They died because of you, Alex."

"Actually, I should have done that but I needed you to help me, or so I thought. I decided I'd give you one more chance," he retorted. "Either you agreed to leave here with me, or—" He pointed the gun toward Lydia and Dr. Haines. "Bang, bang."

"He's posted guards all around us," Paco said on a frustrated hiss. "That's why he wasn't too worried about us escaping."

"How many?" Eli asked from his crouch behind Paco. They'd centered themselves near the lone window of the basement but it was hard to see anything in the growing dusk.

"I count six at least," Shane replied from somewhere in the darkness. "But I only figure that from the ones we've been able to see moving by. Could be more."

"That's only two each, *mon ami*," Eli replied. "We've been in worse jams."

Shane let out a breath. "Yes, that's true. But we have only our wits and our fists to help us in this jam."

Paco couldn't argue with that. Whitmyer had stripped them of their weapons and their phones. "Let's just do this thing so I can get to Laura."

Eli rolled over to stare at him. "What's the plan?"

Paco closed his eyes, said a prayer then forced all the ugly scenarios involving Whitmyer and what he might do to Laura out of his head. "Get their attention, bring 'em in here and then, confuse 'em by gaining control over this situation."

"*Oui,* and how do you propose we do that?" Eli asked.

Paco motioned to them to come close. "There's this black ops tactic we can use and I'm pretty sure it's one Whitmyer failed to mention to his henchmen out there. Listen and learn, boys."

The phone on Laura's bedside table rang.

She glanced at the phone then up at Alex Whitmyer.

"Answer it," he said. "But keep in mind, anything you say can be used against those two." He pointed toward Lydia and the doctor. "I don't have anything to lose if I shoot one or two more people."

Laura put the image of him shooting Paco or any of

the others out of her mind, willing herself to be calm. "Hello," she said into the phone, her voice low and shaky.

"Laura, it's Kissie. The system is jammed and we can't gain access to your wing. Talk to me, baby."

Laura swallowed, trying desperately to show no reaction to the thread of distress in Kissie's words. "Kissie, it's okay. Dr. Haines and Lydia are with me. We're fine."

"Is someone there, honey?"

"Yeah, we were wondering where Selena went. The doctor wants to examine me."

"Selena is across from you in another room. She alerted us when she realized the security code went red."

"Oh, I see. We can wait for her then."

Alex grabbed the phone away then put it to his ear. "Listen to me, and listen good. I've got your patient and the pregnant lady in my gun sight, understand? And if anyone tries to come into this wing, I will shoot the pregnant woman first."

He stood silent then responded to whatever Kissie had said. "Laura? Laura's just fine. She's enjoyed her stay but she'll be leaving with me soon. Goodbye."

He hung up then glanced around. "I think it's time for a change of scenery, Laura. I want you by my side when I take over CSN. I had hoped to make this easy and bring a few CHAIM agents with me, but they don't want to play nice. So we do it the hard way. We start over, you and me."

He tilted his head toward Lydia. "Help her get dressed. And Doc, make sure she's bandaged up. We won't be stopping to dress wounds."

Lydia glared at him. "Where are you taking her?"

He cackled and aimed the gun toward Lydia. "I could tell you, but then I'd have to kill you."

Laura pushed up. "It's okay, Lydia. I'll go with him. Just do as he says." She sent Lydia a pleading look. "I'll be okay."

"I can't let him take you," Lydia said, her voice rising.

"You don't have a choice," Whitmyer retorted, pressing the gun toward Lydia. "If you want to live to deliver that kid, you'd better do as I say, woman."

Laura shook her head. "Lydia, it's all right."

Then Lydia's face went pale as she grabbed her stomach. "It's not all right." A grimace of pain colored her expression. "I think I'm going into labor."

EIGHTEEN

"Divide and conquer," Eli said. "It's been a while since I've had so much fun." Then he rubbed his face. "Except for my sore jaw and black eye, of course."

"Let's hope that's the last of them," Shane retorted, holding the flashlight they'd found so Paco could finish tying up the men who'd been guarding them. "They're down to four now at least. Two of them are no longer breathing."

Eli grunted. "Hey, they came at us first. Strictly self-defense."

"These four aren't going anywhere for a while," Paco said, making sure the knots he tied couldn't be untied. He'd also put tape over the unconscious men's mouths and tape around their legs, too. "Once I tie them all together, it'll take hours for 'em to figure out how to get loose."

"Now to find a phone," Shane said.

"Let's get out of here," Paco retorted, finished with securing the unconscious men.

He waited for Shane and Eli to go out the big steel door then he shut it and wedged a crowbar against it. Just as another precaution.

They did one more search of the estate then found

their guns and phones in a pile in the office where they'd been attacked.

Paco immediately dialed Devon's number.

"Paco? We've been trying to reach you."

He didn't like the tone of Devon's voice. "We ran into some trouble, but that's been taken care of. Is everyone safe and accounted for?"

Devon's hesitation seemed to last a lifetime. "Negative on that. An intruder blocked off the wing where Laura is quartered. We've lost communication and we can't get any visuals. And Lydia's in there with her. They're being held hostage. Selena's hiding in the room next to Laura's but she has her cell with her. She's keeping us updated through text messages. Everyone else is safe for now."

Paco's heart pulsed and pitched then settled into shell shock. "What's the situation?"

"Based on what Selena can glean, one armed man. He apparently jammed the security long enough to force his way inside with Dr. Haines. No news on Andre's condition or his whereabouts. Brice saw the breach and tried to get back in, but the security code blocked access and then the computers went down. Kissie's working to get surveillance back on line. Meantime, we're waiting for another update from Selena. It's too dangerous for us to storm in there." Silence again. "I'm worried about Lydia."

Paco relayed this to Eli and Shane. "We're on our way."

He forced himself to focus on the here and now. He quickly told Devon what had happened with Whitmyer. "It has to be him, Dev. Alex Whitmyer has Laura. He lured me away so he could get to her."

He put away his phone, his blood boiling with anger.

"Why didn't I see this coming?"

Eli pushed a hand in his face. "We move forward and stick to the plan, bro, okay?"

"The plan has changed now," Paco said, shoving him away. "The plan was to get her to safety then find Henner. Well, Henner is nowhere to be found and he's probably dead. We focused on him instead of Whitmyer and so now, the plan has changed."

Shane glanced at Eli then back to Paco. "What *is* the plan now, Warrior?"

Paco grabbed his gun. "To get to Whitmyer before he hurts Laura or anybody else. And to finish this."

"I'm not falling for that one," Whitmyer said, lifting his gun in the air. "I mean it, lady. Don't play games with me."

Laura looked from him to Lydia. "I don't think she's faking. Her baby's due in a couple of weeks."

"Then she needs to hold off on that," Whitmyer retorted. "Check her, Doc. And don't make any stupid moves."

The doctor got up to help Lydia back into her chair. After taking her pulse and asking her a few questions, he held her while another spasm hit her stomach. "This baby is about to be born whether you like it or not."

"Now isn't that just peachy," Whitmyer shouted. Then he smiled. "Well, okay then. I'll take Laura and you can deliver the brat right here in this room. Case closed."

"We can't leave her," Laura said, shaking her head. "I can help."

"She has a doctor for that."

Dr. Haines stood up, reaching a hand to his chest, his flushed face lined with pain. "It's too dangerous. He has a—"

"Stop," Whitmyer shouted, his gun lifting toward the doctor. Laura screamed but it didn't matter. The gun popped, the sound shattering and final.

And then the doctor looked down at the blood spurting from his chest and fell to the floor.

Laura screamed again and got out of bed, her head swimming, her heart pumping as she pulled at her IV drip. She reached toward Lydia, taking her hand. "Hang on, Lydia."

Whitmyer looked as shocked as Laura felt. "There. That's one down and two to go."

"You shot an innocent old man," Laura said, anger giving her the courage to scream. Then she yanked her IV out and got between him and Lydia. "You want me? Well, take me. But stop killing people."

Whitmyer reached toward her but a loud knock at the door stopped him. "Go away," he shouted. "Leave or I shoot another one."

"Let me in there right now. I'm a nurse."

Laura and Lydia glanced at each other. Selena.

Whitmyer shook his head then opened the door and dragged Selena inside. "Just what I need, another aggravating woman." Then he stood still, his harsh gazing moving over the three women. "But, if my notes are correct, two of you are married to CHAIM agents." He glared at Laura. "And one of you obviously has a thing for the mighty Paco Martinez."

Selena took in the scene but didn't say anything. She bent to examine Dr. Haines then looked up, shaking her head. Then she whirled toward Whitmyer. "You made a fatal mistake, taking them hostage. If you think they'll let you get out of this alive, you're wrong." She glanced at Laura. "I need to bandage her arm. It's bleeding."

Whitmyer looked at the spot where Laura's IV had been positioned. "Do it." He held the gun on them while Selena grabbed some gauze and bandages and went to work on Laura's wound.

Selena leaned down close to Laura. "There's blood in the hallway and Andre's missing."

Laura didn't dare react. She stared up at Whitmyer. "She's right. You can't win, Alex."

Whitmyer shrugged, but Laura saw the flash of fear in his eyes. His grand plan was falling apart around him. "I came here for you, Laura. I don't care about the rest."

The phone rang and Laura scrambled to reach it, ignoring Whitmyer's fidgeting. "Hello?" She looked over at him, daring him to shoot her.

"Laura?"

Paco. She didn't dare say his name. "Yes?"

"Are you all right?"

"Yes, but Lydia's going into labor and Dr. Haines is dead. We don't know where Andre is."

Whitmyer stomped toward Selena and Lydia. "Hang up or I'll shoot one of them."

"I have to go," Laura said. "You need to know…."

"I know, sweetheart. You don't have to say anything. I know. You stay strong, you hear me, Laura. I'm coming for you, just like I promised."

Then she heard Brice's clipped words. "Let me speak to him, Laura."

Laura handed the cordless phone toward Whitmyer. "They want to talk to you."

"I'm not making any deals," he said, refusing to take the phone.

"Please?" Laura asked, hoping there was some bit of decency left in the demented man's soul. "For me, Alex. We need to understand why you're doing this. I'll go with you, but at least help me to understand."

Alex hesitated then took the phone, his expression full of rage. "You want to know why I'm holding three women and a dead doctor hostage? I'll tell you. Because I can. Because I've been trained just like all of you, because I gave my life to CSN and Lawrence Henner but he ignored me and focused on his whiny son instead. Then when I offered the deal of a lifetime to all of you, you turned on me, too. So now, it's payback time. Laura is my only hope. Laura understands me. I'm taking her out of here."

He waited, and Laura watched his face, wondering what she'd ever seen in this man. He wasn't rational. She'd dated him when she should have been counseling him. It was way too late to change that. What was Brice saying to him?

"I see. Well, that won't cut it, Mr. Whelan. I can't surrender—and your negotiation tactics won't work. But I do have a request. I want a helicopter out of here. I'm taking Laura Walton with me and if anyone tries to stop me, I'll kill the woman who's in labor and the cute nurse—your wife, I believe—then I'll kill Laura and myself. How's that for negotiations?"

Brice turned to the other men in the room, his hands on his hips. "You heard the man. This could go on for hours."

Devon pushed at his hair and paced. "Lydia's in labor? That is what he indicated, right?"

"Aye," Brice replied, his expression grim. "And now Selena's gone and got herself into the mix, too. We need to alert Kissie that Andre's still missing. That can't be good."

Paco thought about Laura's words to him earlier. Just hearing her voice made him so crazy he wanted to storm the house and tear down that door barring him from her. He understood her message even if she couldn't voice her feelings for him. And he wanted to give her the same message.

He loved her.

Brice went into the computer room next door then came back. "Kissie is trying to get the cameras back online to that section of the house. She's concerned for her son's safety, of course." Brice looked as haggard as Paco felt. "So here's what we have: Security system breached and jammed on south side of the compound due to forced entry using one hostage as cover. That hostage is now dead. Three hostages taken alive. One person missing. Intruder has demands. He wants a helicopter out and he's taking Laura with him."

"Over my dead body," Paco said, slapping his fists together.

"Careful, bro," Eli warned. "We don't need that."

"I can't let him take her," Paco said, staring at his friend. "Do you hear me? I can't let that madman take Laura out of here. You know what that could mean."

Brice nodded. "We understand, Paco. But we have to consider he's also holding Selena and Lydia, too." He glanced toward Devon. "He confirmed that. And Lydia's apparently in labor."

Devon pushed toward the double doors of the war room then turned back around. "I can't take this."

"Selena is with her," Brice said. "In his need to impress, that idiot spilled enough information to help us evaluate the situation and form a plan." He closed his eyes and breathed deep. "We have to focus on that, gentlemen. A plan to get our loved ones out of harm's way."

"Lydia," Devon said. "The baby." He looked at Eli. "I can't let anything happen to them, Eli."

"Nothing will, bro," Eli said. "We're gonna fix this and you'll be a proud papa before sunrise."

Devon didn't look so sure. "Where's Scotty and Gena?"

Eli pointed across the hallway. "They're safe right where we left them—in this wing in the big dining hall with everyone else. Trust me, I've checked on them about three times since we got back."

Shane nodded. "Kit's in there with her parents and the others. Our superiors are well armed and waiting. Meantime, they're all praying and trying to stay calm. Now we need to decide a plan of action. The sooner the better."

Paco whirled around. "We don't have much time before he calls again about the helicopter. Let's get in there and get them out." He looked past the door. "And let's take that psychopath out so he can't hurt anyone else."

"Laura, you need to change clothes."

Laura turned from helping Lydia onto the bed. "I told you, Alex, I'm not leaving her like this. I'll go with you but I don't want to leave Lydia."

He pointed the gun toward Lydia. "And I told you, I don't care about her or that brat."

Lydia grimaced as another round of contractions gripped her stomach. Selena held her hand, talking her through her breathing. "It won't be long now, Lydia. You're doing great."

Lydia used all her angst and agony to stare down Alex Whitmyer. "What kind of man are you?" she shouted between breaths, her knuckles white as she held on to Lydia.

"The kind who takes charge," Whitmyer shot back, grabbing Laura by the arm. "Call Martinez back and tell him we want that helicopter in ten minutes. And don't stall. I know there's at least two choppers on the premises."

Selena shook her head. "Laura can't travel. She's been shot—by someone you sent to harm her."

"I'll get her help as soon as we're out of here."

"You could cause the bleeding to start again or she might go into shock or get an infection."

"I'll take care of her."

Laura glanced from Selena to Whitmyer. She knew what both Selena and Lydia were thinking. If this man took her, her chances of surviving were slim to none. Alex wanted revenge against her and against CHAIM. It was unreasonable and unbelievable, but he wasn't a rational man.

"I'll make the call," she said. She'd convince Paco to give them a helicopter and hope he'd put his sniper skills to good use once they were out in the open.

"Do it." Whitmyer pointed the gun at Lydia. "One wrong word and I'll take mother and baby out of their misery."

God, help me, she prayed. *What should I do?*

Then a thought rushed through her mind. *You're trained to help people like him, Laura. Use that training.*

Somehow, she had to make this look good and then figure out a way to stall him. So she dialed the number to the conference room, her prayers keeping beat with her pulse. She didn't like flying but she had to keep moving, keep hoping that she could find some courage. Blocking nausea, she swallowed back her fears.

Brice answered on the second ring. "Hello?"

"I need to talk to Paco," she said.

"I'll put him on," Brice replied. "I have you on speaker, Laura. So anything you can tell us…"

"Laura, sweetheart, talk to me."

She heard the worry and fear in his words. But she knew this man. He was stronger than he realized. "We need the helicopter. You have ten minutes to get it ready."

"Got it. But you won't be on that chopper. How's Lydia?"

"In labor. Selena's coaching her."

Whitmyer stepped forward. "Enough. Hang up."

Laura glanced at Selena then back to Whitmyer, her fingers touching the button to end the call. Then she put the phone down behind the water pitcher on the table by the bed. And left it on.

Please, Lord, don't let him notice.

"Alex, I promise I'll go with you as soon as the baby is born. Then we can talk. I think I misjudged you."

He shook his head. "It might take all night for that baby to be born. We don't have time, Laura. You have to go with me if you want them to live, understand?"

Laura didn't have a choice. "Okay. The helicopter should be ready soon. But before we go, you need to understand about Paco and me. This isn't his fault."

Whitmyer's gaze darted here and there. "Then why were you traipsing all over Arizona with him? You love me, Laura. You don't love him."

"You're right. I don't love him. I barely know him, but I'm his therapist and I found him so I could talk to him. I can do the same for you. We can get you the help you need."

"I don't need anything, except you to come with me," he shouted, his gun bobbing. "I had this big plan to make CSN into the best—better than CHAIM could ever be. But, I'll give that up just to be with you."

Laura could see the desperation in his eyes. He believed he was in control but he wasn't. And now his misguided delusional scheme had collapsed. She had to make him listen to reason.

"Why did you do all of this, Alex? Why did you send out those inexperienced men to kill me? Why the cryptic messages on my business cards?"

His chuckle sent chills up her spine. "You don't get it, do you, Laura? You belong to me but you wouldn't see me anymore. I had to find a way back to you. I followed you that day, the day you met with Martinez. And I saw you with him. I couldn't take it."

Laura's heart pumped so fast she felt disoriented. "You were at the café in the desert?"

He laughed again, his eyes wild with determination and madness. "I was the first shooter. I wanted to talk to Martinez but when I saw him with you I just wanted to kill him." He shook his head. "Things got crazy after that."

Slanting a look toward Selena and Lydia, Laura took advantage of the precious time. "But what about those other men? Why did they come after me?"

He scoffed, swung the gun around. "Those idiots? It started out with me getting information from your patients since you refused to talk to me. Then I used them as distractions. They wanted to be *somebody*, Laura. They thought if they worked for CSN, they could become security agents. I needed them to believe that so I could keep an eye on you. I brought them with me. They thought it was a training mission.

"But *I* followed you to your hotel and I broke in and got your laptop so I can find out why you were after that loser Martinez. I left the first card for you in the desert but you didn't take the hint. So I fixed up another one and gave it to good ol' Howard and found him a delivery truck. Same with Rutherford—sent him into the desert with promises of a big promotion if he did the job. I knew Martinez would take them out. I knew because I was watching the whole time." He shrugged, his smile smug, his eyes glassy. "I set up the shooter out on the road, too. And I tracked the chopper that brought you to Eagle Rock."

Lydia cried out then, her hand flailing toward the table as another contraction moved through her body. She hit the water pitcher and sent it flying.

Whitmyer whirled toward Lydia, his gaze hitting on the phone's flashing light. Grabbing it, he stared at Laura. "You forgot to hang up?" His expression etched in rage, he held the phone to his ear then pulled her close. "You can never get away from me, Laura. And

Paco Martinez will never have you." He shouted into the receiver. "Hear that, Martinez. You will never have her. Never."

NINETEEN

Paco couldn't breathe.

Never.

That one word followed by a dial tone shouted at him with a laughing glee that seemed to sum up his entire miserable life.

"He's going to kill her," he said, the words dropping out him like rocks hitting concrete.

"We won't let it go that far," Devon replied, his cell phone in his hand. "Mr. Barton is releasing the chopper to you, Paco, because he trusts you to do the right thing. Laura was very brave in risking the open phone line, but she's a counselor. She's trying to talk this man down and give us information at the same time."

"And she's trying to save Lydia and my child," Devon said, a hand on Paco's arm. "I need to get to my wife. I'm just thankful she's still alive."

Paco was thankful for all of that and more. But his heart, once so hard and closed, was now open and raw, exposed to the incredible power of love. He turned to Devon. "He said *never,* Dev. You heard him. This was his plan all along. If he can't have Laura, then no one ever will."

Devon's gaze moved over the others then back to

Paco. "He's a very sick man, Warrior. But we have might on our side. We stay the course."

Eli grunted, his arms crossed over his chest. "There's him and then there's us. I don't think he's gonna make it out of this, *mon ami*. Dev's right. We go by the book on this one."

Paco stared over at his friend. "You tell me how to do that? Tell me how to focus, how to go on faith." He sank down on a chair. "I don't think I can do this. I don't think I can take losing another person I care about. Especially Laura. You don't understand the thing about Laura."

Shane sat down beside him. "We all understand, Paco. We've all fought the good fight for CHAIM. We've worked to save innocents all over the world and sometimes, we've failed at that or worse, we've been forced to take the lives of others. We did that for years, thinking we understood the true meaning of love and faith." He rapped his fingers on the table. "And then, we each got handed these special assignments that changed our whole way of thinking. We love Christ and we believe. But falling in love with someone you want to spend your life with and knowing that very person is in danger—well, that puts a new wrinkle into the whole equation."

"And makes this job unbearable at times," Eli said from his spot against the wall.

Paco's eyes stung. The unfamiliarity of his tears floored him. He'd held these tears for so long and now they burned their way down his face. If he let go now, he'd never make it back. Fighting the pain, he closed his eyes, memories of dust and blood and gunfire covering him. And in those horrid murky memories he could hear a keening, a kind of wailing that shattered his resolve.

He fought against that wailing, against what it meant for him now, on this mission.

Then he opened his eyes and looked at Devon, the pastor. "It was me, man. I was the last one standing and…I saw that kid laying there, dying and I fell down and held him in my arms and…every time I relive that nightmare, I hear this horrible wailing." He put his hands to his face, the tears flowing now. "It was me, Dev. I was wailing at God for doing this. For taking their lives and sparing mine." He grabbed Devon's lapel, his heartbeat bursting through his temples. "I can't take that kind of pain again, man. I can't. What do I do? How do I do this? If I lose Laura—"

"You won't lose Laura," Devon said. "Paco, do you hear me? God is with us even when we fail. Look around you. Look at us. Me, I hid the truth from Eli for years and I almost got Lydia and Eli both killed. Eli—he came back from his own nightmare to find out he had a son in danger because of mistakes from *his* past. He has a reason to live now. Brice was so in love with Selena, he failed to see her worst flaw—her misplaced loyalty to a man who was a criminal. And Shane—he had to fall long and hard before he could get over his fear of a true commitment, not to mention he had to tell the woman he loved her best friend had betrayed her. And that brings me to you, friend. Laura sought you out to help you overcome your post-traumatic stress and survivor's guilt and now you're being tested because of her concern and generosity. Laura believes in you, Paco. We believe in you. And God will see you through—no matter the outcome."

Paco looked around at his friends, memories of all

their times together, memories of their trials and failures, rushing through his mind like an old movie.

"We've done good, haven't we, though?" He waited for Devon to respond.

Eli, Shane and Brice all stepped forward. "Yes, we've done good," Devon replied in a quiet voice. "This can be one of those times, Paco. We're all here with you to make sure of that."

Did he have the power to bring about a hopeful outcome instead of yet another tragedy in his life?

"Laura told me I might have one last mission," he said, wiping at his face. "But she didn't tell me I might fail at that mission. Or that it would be this hard."

"You aren't going to fail," Shane said, grabbing Paco up out of the chair. "You have something to fight for now, Paco. And that means you aren't allowed to fail." He blinked back his own tears, then straightened Paco's jacket. "Now, we're going to get things in order. While you sit here and have a quick talk to the Lord. Understand me?"

Paco nodded. "I don't have much time, do I?"

Devon slapped a hand on his back. "Just enough for the Lord to hear you. Then we take care of this so I can enjoy becoming a father."

Paco waited for the others to leave then took a long breath. Normally in a situation such as this, he'd be the first one out the door—hot dog, hothead, whatever you wanted to call it, he lived for the chase. But that old adrenaline rush had turned into a dreaded beating pulse that lived to torment him.

So he looked up at the intricately woven iron cross centered on the wall, his heart warring between the need for battle and the need for peace. He stared at the cross, taking in the way the iron twisted and turned and merged into itself to form a crossbar of strength.

And in his head, beyond all the tormented memories and the twisted guilt he'd carried for so long, he at last saw the strength forged in fire and steel and blood and tears. The strength of Christ's love guiding him and holding him, even when he'd believed himself to be alone.

"Are You there, Lord?" he asked now, his hands folded in prayer. "I'm not worth it but I need You now. I need You for Laura's sake, Lord. Spare her and I will gladly hand my life over to You. Not a bargain but a promise that I've failed to honor. I love her, Lord. I don't yet understand this love, but I love this woman. And I can't lose her."

He stopped, hitched a breath. "One last mission, Lord. A mission to make up for all the others, to make up for all the loss and the pain and the guilt of my failures."

Paco reached for the Bible that was always on the table, his fingers flipping through the pages. He settled on the book of Psalms, chapter fifty-five, verses four through six:

"'My heart is severely pained within me, and the terrors of death have fallen upon me. Fearfulness and trembling have come upon me, and horror has over-whelmed me. And I said: "Oh, that I had wings like a dove! For then, I would fly away and be at rest."'"

He finished the entire chapter, amazed that some of the very things he felt inside his soul were written here in the Word.

Paco put the Bible down and closed his eyes, his prayers centered and concentrated, his wails of despair changing to silent and steady pleas for God's grace and intervention. Then he opened his eyes and put on the mantle of the Lord so he could join his friends in this fight to save all that they held dear.

Shane and Eli stood back out of sight, watching as Paco went about doing a safety check on the whirling helicopter centered on the landing pad near the back of the big compound. Brice was inside helping Kissie to regain visual surveillance, hoping to make a last-ditch effort to rescue Laura and the others. And Devon was waiting for the go-ahead to break the door down so he could get to his wife before she gave birth.

Paco left the helicopter idling, then hopped out, his thoughts clear now, his on-edge nerve endings humming with purpose. The adrenaline was back, allowing him to keep the dark dread at bay. He had a new hope. And his friends were right. He had a reason to fight one more battle.

Running toward Shane and Eli, Paco did one more scan of the surrounding buildings. "He should be watching," Paco said. "The man has to know I'm going to take him out once he clears the entry door."

They were all geared up for warfare, each wearing a bulletproof vest and loaded with weapons. Shane rubbed his chin. "Of course he's factored that in, but he'll use Laura as a shield. He'll lock Selena and Lydia in the room then bring Laura out the passageway to the same door he entered with Dr. Haines. Still can't figure how he beat the system."

"He's obviously an expert at security," Eli retorted. "He's gone overboard with this obsessive need to take over the world and get the girl."

"It might be different if the man actually knew the

difference between right and wrong," Shane said, his tone murderous. "But a jilted stalker who has grandiose ideas about how to run a company is an unstable person to begin with, so this could be tricky to the bitter end."

Paco checked the high-powered sniper rifle he'd taken from the weapons closet. "I only need one shot."

"Better make it a good one, bro," Eli said.

Paco intended to do that. It would be a kill shot.

Laura held Lydia's hand on one side while Selena spoke to Lydia with soothing words on the other.

"You're doing great," Selena said. "Your breathing is right on target."

"The baby?" Lydia asked, her voice raw, tears of frustration streaming down her face. "Selena, what about my baby?"

Selena's smile was practiced and serene. "As far as I can tell, the baby is right on target, too. You're not quite there yet, though. You need to dilate a few more centimeters."

Lydia nodded. "I'm trying to hold off. I want Devon to be here."

Laura sent Alex Whitmyer a hard look. "Devon will be here soon, honey."

Alex rolled his eyes and flexed his gun. "He won't if they don't call about that chopper."

The phone rang a second later, jarring all of them into a nervous twitter. Laura picked it up, her heart doing laps against her ribs. "Yes?"

"The helicopter is ready," Paco told her. "Laura, listen very carefully. I'm going to be watching. We're all watching. And I'm going to get you out of this."

"I understand," she said. She wanted to say so much more, but she didn't. She couldn't. Her one prayer shouted for God to watch over these people. And to help Alex, too.

And then Alex motioned for her to hand him the phone.

"Martinez? You don't want to make that shot, understand?"

Laura met Selena's knowing gaze as they listened. Had he heard what Paco had said?

"I'm not stupid," Alex shouted into the phone. "You're trained to do this so I expected it. But I've left one little surprise for everyone here at Eagle Rock. And if you kill me, that surprise will blow up in your face, understand? I'm taking her out of here and there's nothing you can do to stop me."

He hung up the phone then went into action. Motioning to Selena and Lydia, he said, "You two will have to stay in here and birth that baby, I'm afraid. I'm going to lock the door. They know where you are, but they might not make it in here to help you."

He didn't elaborate but Laura got a sick feeling inside her stomach as he urged her toward the door. Alex Whitmyer wasn't through with CHAIM yet.

Paco hung up the phone then looked at the group. "He's planted a bomb."

Kissie rushed out the side door and hurried to where they were hiding behind a garage fence, her eyes wild, tears streaming down her face. "It's Andre, Paco. He made Dr. Haines strap a bomb on my baby boy." She grabbed Paco's arm then turned toward Eli. "Eli…"

Eli took her into a hug, looking over her shoulder at Paco. "He probably set it to go off after he's up in the air."

Paco looked at the chopper then back to Eli. "Or to go off if he's shot. He could have the detonator centered somewhere on his body."

Kissie lifted away from Eli, wiping her eyes. "You can't shoot him, Paco. This whole place will go up."

"How did you discover the bomb?" Shane asked Kissie.

"I got the cameras back up," Kissie said, then she shook her head. "No, *I* didn't. He must have a remote jamming the system covering that wing of the compound. He brought the surveillance back online so I'd see my baby strapped to a chair with a bomb ticking on his chest."

Eli took Kissie by the shoulders. "Where is Andre?"

"In the chapel," Kissie replied. "Inside the wing where he's been holding the others. I reckon no one thought to go in there to pray today."

"Here they come," Devon said, turning toward the chopper.

Paco watched Whitmyer and Laura moving toward the helicopter. He had Laura on his left side, using her as a shield. She looked scared but even from this distance Paco could see the resolve in her expression.

Then the house phone he'd brought out here rang again.

"Can you see us?" Whitmyer asked, flashing a grin.

"I see you."

"Good. Now here's your dilemma, Martinez. By now,

you know where that kid Andre is and you also know that he has a bomb ticking right along with his heart. I can deactivate the bomb at anytime by hitting a button on my watch, but I'm giving you a choice here. You can take me out and save Laura, but everyone inside that big house will die. Or you can let me take her and save Andre and the rest of your band of brothers. It's your choice. I'll give you exactly one minute to decide what kind of hero you want to be."

TWENTY

Laura gasped, her stomach roiling with nausea. Her prayers skidded and careened inside her head. Andre had a bomb strapped on him? And Alex was asking Paco to make a choice.

There was no choice. Paco had to save the others.

"Alex," she said, trying to turn so she could see his face. "You don't have to do this. I'm going with you."

He yanked her arm, causing her to cry out. "You don't want to be with me though, do you? You'd rather be with that renegade soldier. I hear he's just about as crazy as I am but I guess I'm not as charming as him, huh?"

Laura knew all the correct answers but nothing in her training had prepared her for this. How many would die here today if she didn't stop this? She thought about Gerald and Sally Mae Barton and Mr. and Mrs. Simpson and the Andersons. She thought about Shane and Katherine happily planning their second wedding just so they could repeat their vows. And Eli laughing as he tossed his son Scotty up into his arms and dangled him by his feet until the boy cackled with laughter. She thought about how Brice loved to recite sonnets to Selena and how she smiled each time he walked by.

Then she thought about Devon, waiting to hear word on Lydia and his child. Their love was so strong, so secure.

Then she thought about Paco. This would destroy him. He would have a breakdown. And this time, he might not recover.

"Alex, we can start over. Just you and me. I promise I'll listen to you. We had a good thing. I just didn't see how much you loved me before."

"Oh, so you get that now!" His harsh laughter indicated he really didn't care. "Time's up. Your man Martinez didn't want to join up with me at CSN so now he has to make a choice."

Laura touched a hand to Alex's face. "No, Alex, you don't understand. You have a choice to do what's right. *You* have to show me you can be the kind of man I'll respect and admire by letting these people live. And in return, I'll willingly go with you and we'll figure this out."

He stared down at her, then put his hand over hers, his expression softening. "I do love you, Laura."

"And I love you," she replied, asking God to keep her calm. "It'll be all right, Alex. I promise."

Paco had them in his sights. He could get this over with and done right now but he couldn't take the shot. Sweat poured down his forehead and pooled between his shoulder blades. His fingers felt sticky against the metal of the rifle. He watched as Laura reached up to touch Whitmyer's cheek, watched as the man looked down at her.

What was she doing?

Brice called from the house. Shane held his phone

so Paco could hear. "Eli and I both think we can get to Andre. The bomb's ticking but the timer's not set. If we can get in there, I'm pretty sure I could deactivate the bomb before he hits the remote timer."

"We don't have time to deactivate the bomb, Whelan," Paco said, wiping sweat with his sleeve. "*My* minute's up."

The house phone rang again. Paco dropped his rifle. "Whitmyer—"

"It's me, Paco."

Laura.

He swallowed, took another breath. "Are you all right?"

"I will be," she said, her words low, her voice strained. "Paco, I'm going with him. I'm going with him and as soon as we're in the air, he's going to deactivate the bomb and you'll all be safe."

"No, Laura. No. He told *me* I had to decide. We can figure this out, sweetheart. Just give me some time."

"There is no time. I'm going with Alex and everything will be fine."

"Laura, it won't be fine. He'll kill you. He's insane and he won't let you go. Ever. Do you understand?"

"Yes," she said. "But Paco, God and I, we believe in you. Remember that. I have to go now."

The line went dead. Paco picked up the gun, rage filling his soul. That lunatic had used her guilt and her generosity to seal the deal. And Paco was helpless to do anything about it. All he could do was watch through his rifle scope while Laura ducked low under the chopper's rudders and waited as Whitmyer lifted her up into the chopper.

And then, Paco saw it. He knew what he had to do to save Laura. He turned to Shane. "I have a new plan. And this one won't fail."

Laura hurt all over. Her breath hit at her ribs, reminding her that she still had a wound in her shoulder. Her insides roiled, not so much from the pain radiating across her body. But mostly from the sheer terror she felt about getting into this helicopter. She'd been blissfully unconscious when they brought her in.

She wouldn't look down. She'd never gotten close to the edge of any cliff or any high windows. She'd always taken the aisle seat on airplanes and that, only after she'd run out of other travel options. But she could do this. Her prayers asked for courage and protection, her heart hurt for the agony of leaving Paco behind.

"Dear God, give us all strength, show us Your grace, allow us Your redemption."

"You think prayers will solve everything, don't you?"

Laura opened her eyes to find Alex staring over at her, a smug look on her face. "Yes, I do. You should try it sometime."

He laughed, his hands working the controls. "I learned a long time ago I can't rely on God for anything."

Hoping to understand, Laura pushed. "What happened to you, Alex?"

He shook his head. "Too late for therapy now."

He lifted the bird into the air, the process shaky.

"Do you know how to fly this thing?" Laura asked in a loud voice, a new fear surfacing. If they crashed, the bomb might still go off.

"Like riding a bike, baby," Alex shouted. Then he

motioned for her to put on her headphones. "Mr. Henner trained me to fly both choppers and light planes."

"What happened to Mr. Henner?" she asked to distract herself, the drone of the chopper muffled for now.

"He and I had a disagreement," Alex replied through the static in her ears. "He lost."

"I think he was a good man but he never got over his son's death."

Alex gave her a thumbs-up. "No, he didn't. But you see, Laura. He had *two* sons. Nobody knew it but him and me—happened before he married and had Kyle. After my mother died, he reluctantly took care of me and later, brought me into the company. But he could never see my potential. He ignored me all of my life. But not anymore. Not this time."

Shocked and appalled but understanding his motives at last, Laura braced herself as the chopper whirled through the air. Taking deep breaths, she held to her prayers and her training. "Alex, you promised you'd deactivate the bomb, remember?"

He checked several gauges and buttons. "What if I lied about that?"

Laura cried out, trembles moving through her body. "You promised, Alex. Don't be like your father. You can't hurt those people."

"Watch me."

And then, she caught a movement out of the corner of her eye, behind them.

Paco swept a hand around to Whitmyer's throat, a thick nasty-looking knife centered on his Adam's apple. Yanking off the headphones, he shouted, "He's not going to hurt anyone, ever again, sweetheart."

Whitmyer pointed toward his watch, but Paco pushed the knife close enough to draw blood. "One move and you die, Whitmyer. Now take off the watch very slowly and hand it to Laura."

Whitmyer shook his head. The chopper spiraled and whirled.

Dizziness hit Laura. She gritted her teeth against it.

"We'll all die together," Whitmyer shouted above the deafening noise, his eyes wild. "How about that?"

Paco let out a grunt, twisted his hand around the man's neck and watched as Whitmyer passed out. Then he went into action, dragging Whitmyer out of the pilot's seat. "Laura, undo his watch while I land this chopper."

"What about the bomb?" she asked, frantically trying to unbuckle the black band.

"If I know Brice, he's already subdued the bomb but we have to make sure we turn off that detonator to be sure. And that's what I need you to do right now."

Laura slid the watch off of Alex's limp wrist. "Which button?"

Paco held on to the controls, steadying the big bird, his gaze moving over the dial. "The red button on the left should do the trick."

Laura prayed he was right. She pushed at the button, her hands trembling and shaking with each jolt of the chopper. Then she heard a beep, beep, beep and held her breath as she finally looked out the window toward Eagle Rock.

The beeps stopped. Laura closed her eyes, terrified she'd hear an explosion from below.

Then Paco touched her hand. "You can open your eyes now, sweetheart. We're headed for solid ground."

Laura looked down and cried out with delight. Kissie stood waving to them, Andre by her side.

"He's in custody," Paco told Laura two hours later. "And we're to head into Austin tomorrow to give a full report." He reached for her hand. "You don't have to go. The authorities will get your statement when you're feeling better."

Laura didn't know if she'd ever feel better. But having him alive and nearby did help. She still couldn't believe he'd hitched a ride on a chopper leg and crawled through the open door into the back of the chopper undetected to stop Whitmyer.

"And everyone else?"

"They're all relieved and celebrating their blessings. I think Mrs. Barton and the other ladies are cooking up a feast."

"*Our* blessings," she corrected.

He looked confused.

"We're all counting our blessings, Paco. And you're the number one blessing on my list."

He let go of her hand then walked over to the window. She was now in a plush bedroom in the main part of the house. "I don't consider myself a blessing to anyone."

"Your grandfather thinks you're a blessing. He wasn't even surprised when we called to tell him the news that we were both safe. He knew you'd take care of business."

Now that his business was finished, would he leave her here? He was already putting distance between them.

He turned to stare down at her, his expression caught

between acceptance and resistance. "I have a long way to go, Laura. It won't be easy. I'm not an easy man."

"I have a whole lifetime to wait for you, Paco."

He came over to her and lifted her into his arms. "Would you wait that long for me?"

"I think I might," she said, snuggling against him. Maybe it was the pain meds, or maybe it was the warmth of his arms, but she felt drowsy with happiness.

"We've got a lot to sort through," he said. "Whitmyer left a long trail of dead bodies and it'll take months to clean up this case."

Laura nodded. "I can't believe he killed Mr. Henner—his own father—and buried him on his ranch. And I can't imagine what kind of warped relationship those two had. It's so sad, so horrible."

"Whitmyer is a very sick man, Laura. He hid it well. But he's going to be locked away a long, long time. Seeking revenge, he took advantage of Henner's grief and your guilt in an attempt to change CSN into a killing machine. He might have compared himself to CHAIM but I pray none of us are like him."

Laura looked up at him. "No, you're not like him. And that's why I won't ever give up on you, Paco."

There was a knock on the door. "Come in," Laura called. Paco got up to see who it was.

Devon wheeled in Lydia. And she was holding their little girl.

Tears sprang to Laura's eyes as she looked at the tiny bundle Lydia held in her arms. "Oh, she's so beautiful."

Devon grinned. "Yes, she is. I think she looks like her mother."

Laura smiled up at him. "I hear you made it just in time."

"Yes. Just in time," Devon said, nodding toward Paco.

Lydia shot Laura a thankful look. "You were so brave today, Laura. You and Selena got me through this."

Laura looked over at Paco. "It's been a long day, and I'm so thankful it's over."

Devon glanced at his friend. "It's almost dinner time. You two coming or do you want a tray here in your room?"

"We'll be there in a few minutes," Paco said.

Laura grinned at Lydia. "Oh, what did you name the baby?"

Lydia smiled up at Devon. "I had planned on naming her Scarlett, but we came up with a better name. Lana. It's a cross between Laura and Selena."

"And it has an *L* to remind us of Luke," Devon added with a wink.

Paco actually grinned back at them. "That's kind of cool."

After they left, he came and sat down in the chair by Laura, took her hand then lowered his head. "I want you to know...today when I thought I was going to lose you, I prayed, Laura. I prayed so hard and I turned my life over to Christ. I mean, really turned my life over to Christ. I promised Him I'd serve Him if He only let you live."

Laura touched a hand to his head. "Paco, God knew you had already been serving him. He knew your heart and your pain when you were holding that soldier on that mountaintop. It's all right. You're going to be all right now."

He looked up at her. "How did you get so wise?"

She smiled. "I'm not that wise. But I believe in the power of God's love and healing."

He tugged her close and kissed her. "This won't be our last kiss, you know."

"I sure hope not."

"It might take a while, but I believe I can make you happy."

"I'm already happy," she said. "I love you."

He stared at her as if he'd never heard those words before. "I love you, too." Then he kissed her again. "If I were to ask you to maybe marry me one day, what would you say?"

Tears streamed down her face. "I'd probably say yes."

He kissed her again. "And if I were to ask you where you'd like to go on our honeymoon, what would you say?"

She touched her hands to his face and smiled. "I'd say, let's go to the Grand Canyon."

"You're kidding, right?"

"No," she replied. "I think I'm finally ready to get close to the edge."

He pulled her up and held her, his gaze moving over her face. "You are an amazing woman, Laura Walton."

"Don't you forget it, Paco Martinez."

A few minutes later, Gerald Barton stood at the head of a long table, his smile proud, his eyes misty. "We started CHAIM all those years ago to do good in this world, to serve the Lord in battle and to protect Christians who needed our help. We've made mistakes and lost a few fights, but we're still here and we're still kicking. And tonight, after all the hoopla and excitement, and now that we have our own Laura back safe and sound, we raise our voices in thanks to five brave men—Devon Malone, the pastor, Eli Trudeau, the disciple, Brice Whelan, the shepherd, Shane Warwick, the knight, and Paco Martinez, the warrior. We thank each of you for your service."

Then Delton Carter stood. "And in light of the events that brought us all here tonight and in light of how these young warriors have changed into strong family men, we'd like to announce a new venture. We want the five of you to run a brand-new branch of CHAIM."

"I'm retired," Devon reminded him with a smile.

"I'm thinking about opening a fishing charter in Grand Isle," Eli said.

"I'm going back to Whelan Castle," Brice shouted out.

"And I'm going to remarry the woman I love," Shane reminded them.

They all looked at Paco. He took Laura's hand and glanced around the room. "I'm going to show this woman that I can be a good husband and... I haven't thought much beyond that."

Everyone clapped, but Delton raised a hand for quiet. "This venture will be different. We'll still be security, but we'll mainly market and sell a line of security products for business and homes. Safe, honest work, but with a bit of challenge now and then."

The agents all stared at each other then Eli shrugged. "*Oui*, and how long do you think that will last, Delton?"

Delton grinned and reached for the carving knife.

Looking at the big turkey waiting to be cut, he said, "Oh, it was worth a try, right, fellows! And anyway, my wife suggested it."

Everyone started laughing at once. Then the food was blessed and passed around the table.

Laura looked over at Paco and smiled. Then she reached up to touch his chest. "You've found your heart, Paco."

He nodded, kissed her fingers then leaned over to kiss her. "Yes, and I'm looking at it."

Shane raised his water glass then winked at Paco. "Mission accomplished."

* * * * *

Dear Reader:

This is a bittersweet book for many reasons. It's the last in my CHAIM series of secret agents. Who knew that one workshop at a conference would bring about five different stories! I'll miss these characters but...maybe one day I can revisit CHAIM and see how things are going.

I actually got the idea for this book from a dream where a soldier came to me and told me his father died in Vietnam, his brother was wounded in Desert Storm and he'd just returned from Iraq. He said he needed someone to talk to. I woke up crying and jotted down his request. And this is his story. This is a story of every soldier who is hurting or afraid. Luke needed someone to talk with, but he was so afraid of letting go of all the horror of war. Laura Walton wanted to help Luke but she learned a few valuable lessons along the way. And she slowed him how to love again. When I researched this story, I found a poem about a heart hunter. It talked about a man who went around searching for a true heart—he wanted to understand why things happen and he wanted to find love so he could feel his heart beating again. I think Luke was such a man. And I'm so glad that he found his heart again.

Thank you for going on this adventure with me. Let me know what you think by visiting my website at www.lenoraworth.com. I love hearing from readers.

Until next time, may the angels watch over you. Always.

Lenora Worth

QUESTIONS FOR DISCUSSION

1. Why did Luke call Laura on the hotline? Have you ever had such a midnight call in your life?

2. Was Laura right to track down Luke? Did she go too far?

3. Why do you think Luke turned away from Laura at first? Have you known someone who held all emotion inside? How did you help that person?

4. Laura's faith kept her centered. Her presence calmed Luke. Do you have someone like this in your life?

5. Luke loved his family but it seemed they had a bleak life. Have you overcome adversity in your life? How did your faith help?

6. Laura liked helping people through emotional crisis but this often caused her to see the worst in people. How do you deal with friend or family in crisis?

7. Soldiers often hold in the things they experience during war. How can we help them?

8. Do you know someone like Luke? Have you experienced some of the same emotions and frustrations as Laura?

9. Luke was trained to kill. Soldiers have to deal with this on a daily basis. Do you think being a Christian makes this even harder for a soldier?

10. The CHAIM team was very close. How did this closeness help Luke in the end?

11. The women who loved these men learned how to deal with a lot of danger and uncertainty. Is there a lesson there for all of us?

12. Did you like the ending of this book? Do you think the CHAIM team will ever break up and take on different careers?

Love Inspired®
SUSPENSE

TITLES AVAILABLE NEXT MONTH

Available January 11, 2011

When Texas Ranger Benjamin Fritz arrives at his captain's house after receiving an urgent message, he finds him murdered and the man's daughter in shock.

Read on for a sneak peek at DAUGHTER OF TEXAS by Terri Reed, the first book in the exciting new TEXAS RANGER JUSTICE series, available January 2011 from Love Inspired Suspense.

Corinna's dark hair had loosened from her normally severe bun. And her dark eyes were glassy as she stared off into space. Taking her shoulders in his hands, Ben pulled her to her feet. She didn't resist. He figured shock was setting in.

When she turned to face him, his heart contracted painfully in his chest. "You're hurt!"

She didn't seem to hear him.

Blood seeped from a scrape on her right upper biceps. He inspected the wound. Looked as if a bullet had grazed her. Whoever had killed her father had tried to kill her. With aching ferocity, rage roared through Ben. The heat of the bullet cauterized the flesh. It would probably heal quickly enough.

But Ben had a feeling that her heart wouldn't heal anytime soon. She'd adored her father. That had been apparent from the moment Ben set foot in the Pike world. She'd barely tolerated Ben from the get-go, with her icy stares and brusque manner, making it clear she thought him not good enough to be in her world. But when it came to her father...

Greg had known that if anything happened to him, she'd need help coping with the loss.

Ben, I need you to promise me if anything ever happens to me, you'll watch out for Corinna. She'll need an anchor.

I fear she's too fragile to suffer another death.

Of course Ben had promised. Though he'd refused to even allow the thought to form that any harm would befall his mentor and friend. He'd wanted to believe Greg was indestructible. But he wasn't. None of them were.

The Rangers were human and very mortal, performing a risky job that put their lives on the line every day.

Never before had Ben been so acutely aware of that fact.

Now his captain was gone. It was up to him not only to bring Greg's murderer to justice, but to protect and help Corinna Pike.

For more of this story, look for DAUGHTER OF TEXAS by Terri Reed, available in January 2011 from Love Inspired Suspense.

REQUEST YOUR FREE BOOKS!

2 FREE RIVETING INSPIRATIONAL NOVELS
PLUS 2 FREE MYSTERY GIFTS

YES! Please send me 2 FREE Love Inspired® Suspense novels and my 2 FREE mystery gifts (gifts are worth about $10). After receiving them, if I don't wish to receive any more books, I can return the shipping statement marked "cancel". If I don't cancel, I will receive 4 brand-new novels every month and be billed just $4.24 per book in the U.S. or $4.74 per book in Canada. That's a saving of 20% off the cover price. It's quite a bargain! Shipping and handling is just 50¢ per book.* I understand that accepting the 2 free books and gifts places me under no obligation to buy anything. I can always return a shipment and cancel at any time. Even if I never buy another book, the two free books and gifts are mine to keep forever.

123/323 IDN E7QZ

Name _____
(PLEASE PRINT)

Address _____ Apt. #

City _____ State/Prov. _____ Zip/Postal Code

Signature (if under 18, a parent or guardian must sign)

Mail to **Steeple Hill Reader Service:**
IN U.S.A.: P.O. Box 1867, Buffalo, NY 14240-1867
IN CANADA: P.O. Box 609, Fort Erie, Ontario L2A 5X3

Not valid for current subscribers to Love Inspired Suspense books.

Want to try two free books from another series?
Call 1-800-873-8635 or visit www.morefreebooks.com.

* Terms and prices subject to change without notice. Prices do not include applicable taxes. Sales tax applicable in N.Y. Canadian residents will be charged applicable provincial taxes and GST. Offer not valid in Quebec. This offer is limited to one order per household. All orders subject to approval. Credit or debit balances in a customer's account(s) may be offset by any other outstanding balance owed by or to the customer. Please allow 4 to 6 weeks for delivery. Offer available while quantities last.

Your Privacy: Steeple Hill Books is committed to protecting your privacy. Our Privacy Policy is available online at www.SteepleHill.com or upon request from the Reader Service. From time to time we make our lists of customers available to reputable third parties who may have a product or service of interest to you. If you would prefer we not share your name and address, please check here. ☐

Help us get it right—We strive for accurate, respectful and relevant communications. To clarify or modify your communication preferences, visit us at www.ReaderService.com/consumerschoice.

LISUS10R

Love Inspired SUSPENSE

RIVETING INSPIRATIONAL ROMANCE

TEXAS RANGER JUSTICE

Keeping the Lone Star State safe

Follow the men and women of the Texas Rangers,
as they risk their lives to help save others,
with

DAUGHTER OF TEXAS by **Terri Reed**
January 2011

BODY OF EVIDENCE by **Lenora Worth**
February 2011

FACE OF DANGER by **Valerie Hansen**
March 2011

TRAIL OF LIES by **Margaret Daley**
April 2011

THREAT OF EXPOSURE by **Lynette Eason**
May 2011

OUT OF TIME by **Shirlee McCoy**
June 2011

Available wherever books are sold.

Steeple Hill®

www.SteepleHill.com

LISCONT11